If he shut down every slightest twinge of connection, how would his daughter ever learn to open her heart again?

"All fixed." Ian waved the screwdriver toward the window. "Nothing's going to sneak in here and surprise you."

"Thank you so much." Relief was written all over Rachel's lovely face.

Ian's chest stirred again, and he realized what he'd begun to feel was more than simple connection. More than just a protective streak. He knew that ache. It had just been a long, long time since it had wrapped itself around his battered heart.

Rachel tucked a stray curl of shimmering auburn hair behind her ear, seemingly oblivious to the effect she had on him. Why, oh why, did it have to be her? "I'll sleep better tonight for sure."

Ian forced a smile. *That makes one of us.*

Dear Reader,

Thank you so much for picking up a copy of *A Double Dose of Happiness*! I am thrilled to be part of the second Harlequin Special Edition Furever Yours pet rescue continuity series. Pets have been near and dear to my heart all my life, and I love doing anything I can to encourage helping animals. At its heart, this is a story that celebrates the special bond between people and their pets. I hope it brings you all the warm fuzzies when you read it, because I certainly enjoyed writing every word.

Rachel Gray and Ian Parsons are both facing difficult circumstances in their lives, and caring for rescue cat Salty and his sweet BFF rescue dog, Pepper, help them learn to open their hearts to love again—both the unconditional love of a pet and romantic love, as well. Salty and Pepper also help Ian's young daughters, Abby and Annie, deal with grieving the loss of their mother.

It's my sincerest wish that reading about Salty and Pepper and their new family brings you a feeling of hope and optimism. I'm imagining readers curled up under a blanket with a dog or cat (or maybe even both) at their feet as they flip these pages.

Happy reading and thank you again for choosing this book!

Best wishes,

Teri

A Double Dose of Happiness

TERI WILSON

HARLEQUIN
SPECIAL
EDITION

Special thanks and acknowledgment are given to Teri Wilson
for her contribution to the Furever Yours miniseries.

HARLEQUIN®
SPECIAL
EDITION™

Recycling programs
for this product may
not exist in your area.

ISBN-13: 978-1-335-72402-1

A Double Dose of Happiness

Copyright © 2022 by Harlequin Enterprises ULC

For questions and comments about the quality of this book,
please contact us at CustomerService@Harlequin.com.

Harlequin Enterprises ULC
22 Adelaide St. West, 41st Floor
Toronto, Ontario M5H 4E3, Canada
www.Harlequin.com

Printed in U.S.A.

Teri Wilson is a *Publishers Weekly* bestselling author of romance and romantic comedy. Several of Teri's books have been adapted into Hallmark Channel Original Movies, most notably *Unleashing Mr. Darcy*. She is also a recipient of the prestigious RITA® Award for excellence in romance fiction for her novel *The Bachelor's Baby Surprise*. Teri has a major weakness for cute animals and pretty dresses, and she loves following the British royal family. Visit her at www.teriwilson.net.

Visit the Author Profile page
at Harlequin.com for more titles.

For all the shelter dogs and cats out there
still waiting for a forever home.
May your day come soon.

Chapter One

"How can my kid be behind in school when she's not even three years old yet?"

Ian Parsons felt another headache coming on—a Baby Einstein, toddler Mensa-induced rager of a headache. Wasn't preschool supposed to be fun?

"I think maybe you've misunderstood." Marianne Foster, the director of the Spring Forest Day School, gazed at Ian serenely from the other side of her desk. Serenity aside, he still felt like a teenager who'd been called into the principal's office and was about to get expelled. "When I say Annie is falling behind, I'm not talking about schoolwork. I mean that she's behind her peers developmentally."

Right, because that's so much better.

"She's become quite withdrawn lately, and when she does speak, it's often in baby talk," Marianne said, whispering the last two words as if they were far too horrible to say out loud.

Ian shifted in his chair. He'd noticed the baby talk thing. But honestly, was it really that big of a deal? Annie was only two and a half. It was sort of cute. And after what his twin girls had been through in their short lives, a little baby talk or thumb-sucking was understandable.

In the first few months after Serena passed away, Ian himself had felt like curling into the fetal position on the floor on more than one occasion. He wasn't sure how baby talk helped Annie—but he wasn't a psychologist and he wasn't going to argue with anything that helped his daughter cope. Because they were talking about coping mechanisms, weren't they? That's what all these sorts of behaviors were. Ian would have been more concerned if Annie hadn't shown any outward signs of reacting to all of the struggles their little family had been dealing with in the past year.

"She is a baby," Ian said, smoothing down his tie. "And I'm not going to stand in the way of her expressing herself in whatever way is most comfortable to her."

That's right, lady. I'm a widowed father of twin

toddlers who works fifty hours a week and still makes time to read parenting books.

What choice did he have? Without the advice of his bookshelf full of literary Mary Poppinses, along with all those annoyingly cheerful Baby Einstein videos, Ian wouldn't have the first clue what he was doing. He still didn't, truth be told.

But he tried. Even now, after a full day at the office of the civil engineering firm where Ian was a senior partner, the words to Abby and Annie's favorite educational song—the one about rocket ships—spun through his mind on constant repeat. Ian didn't spend his free time on the golf course or at Pins and Pints—the local bar/bowling alley—like his work friends did. He made an effort, and he possessed enough book knowledge to know that the term *baby* could be used to describe any child from birth to four years old.

Nevertheless, Marianne arched a judgmental eyebrow at him. "The point is that your daughter is regressing. To be honest, they both are. Just yesterday, Abby intentionally knocked down a tower of blocks that one of her classmates built."

"And?" Ian prompted.

Wasn't that what happened with block towers? If not, wouldn't the world be littered with stacks of blocks far and wide?

"And—" Marianne huffed dramatically *"—the* other child was quite upset. There were tears."

Again, they were toddlers. Weren't tears perfectly normal with this age group? Should he have put his engineering skills to work and constructed a fence to surround said block tower?

"You make Abby sound like a toddler-sized Godzilla," he said flatly.

Marianne's eyebrow arched even higher. If she didn't realign her features, Ian was going to lose it.

"Back to Annie," she said. *Thank God.* "It seems she's taken a step backward in her mobility skills, as well."

Ian's response was a blank stare. He had no idea what she was talking about, but he wished she'd talk about it faster and get to the point—if she actually had one. He hadn't expected to be called into the principal's office when he'd arrived to pick up the twins at the end of the school day. He just wanted to get out of this office, go home and do something normal. Something non-angst ridden, like dining on dinosaur-shaped chicken nuggets for dinner. Or maybe the girls could ride their matching pink tricycles around the cul-de-sac in their quiet, wooded neighborhood in the Kingdom Creek development. Abby could point out the Lost Cat flyers that she'd become so obsessed with. They dotted almost every lamppost in Spring Forest, courtesy of a very determined nine-year-old Brooklyn Hobbs, who'd been inconsolable since her cat wandered off. Ian was mildly surprised that he hadn't started seeing Oliver Hobbs's orange tabby face in his sleep.

"Perhaps you've noticed that Annie has regressed to crawling rather than walking?" Marianne said, dragging his attention back to the matter at hand.

"What?" Ian shook his head. "No."

That just wasn't possible. He would have noticed if one of his daughters had stopped walking. Sure, Annie liked to pretend she was a dog sometimes and move around on all fours, but that seemed perfectly logical to Ian. He'd never met a dog who walked on his hind legs on a regular basis. Frankly, that sounded creepy—far more disturbing than a toddler who dabbled in baby talk and puppy role-play.

Marianne ignored his objection. Ian was starting to believe that the director of his children's day care center had an agenda, and he wasn't altogether sure he wanted to know what it was.

"I understand that things have been difficult at home. It's perfectly natural for the twins to be struggling, but if things don't improve soon, we might have to consider an alternative arrangement," she said.

Every muscle in Ian's body tensed. "You're not seriously considering *expelling* my daughters, are you?"

Had she lost her mind? They were two-year-olds. And even if Abby had gotten a little aggressive with block towers, surely that wasn't enough to warrant expulsion.

"No." She gave him another serene smile that made Ian think she had one of those mini Zen gardens tucked into a desk drawer somewhere. He had a sudden urge to find it and snap the tiny rake in two. "We believe Abby can still function well in the classroom, but we'd like you to consider sending Annie elsewhere so she can receive the dedicated, individualized help she needs."

Ian gripped the arms of the chair he was sitting on so hard that his knuckles turned white. "You want to *separate* the girls? Absolutely not."

Never. Abby and Annie had lost their mother. He wasn't about to let them lose each other. His twins did everything together. They'd never understand why they needed to attend separate schools.

Serena is probably rolling in her grave right now. In her last days, Ian had promised his wife he would do his best to give their girls a happy childhood. He'd sworn. And now here he was, just a year after Serena's funeral, on the verge of being an epic parental failure.

Marianne folded her hands neatly in front of her, clearly unfazed by Ian's unraveling. "Mr. Parsons, everyone here at Spring Forest Day School only wants what's best for Annie, I assure you."

"What's best is *not* separating her from her sister. I'd pull both girls out of this school before I let that happen." Ian stood. He couldn't keep having this discussion.

How on earth am I going to explain this madness to Elma?

His mother-in-law was well-meaning, but like most mothers-in-law, Elma had strong opinions about how her grandchildren should be raised. Those feelings had only grown in intensity since Serena's passing. If Elma had her way, Annie and Abby would stay with her on weekdays when Ian went to work, playing in their mother's old room. Serena's childhood bedroom was still perfectly preserved in all of its gingham-ruffled glory. The only change Elma had made was to remove the grand canopy bed and replace it with twin beds for the girls. Annie and Abby felt perfectly at home there.

Too at home, as far as Ian was concerned. He knew Elma missed her daughter, but that didn't give the woman the right to commandeer her granddaughters to fill that gap. They were still *his* children, after all, and he wanted to be the person who raised them. Serena's dying wish had been for her girls to have a normal and happy childhood. Happy, well-adjusted kids had friends, and that's why Ian wanted the girls in preschool, interacting with other kids their age, instead of at Elma's house during the day.

A little healthy distance from his mother-in-law couldn't hurt, either, though. It was hard to be a good dad when he felt like Elma was constantly looking over his shoulder. But this...

This was different. This was *serious*. If Elma got wind of the fact that Annie was on the verge of expulsion, Ian was toast.

"Mr. Parsons, please sit down." Marianne waved a hand at the chair he'd just vacated. Her tone was as tranquil as ever. It made Ian want to roar. "Maybe if we just calm down—"

He glared at Marianne. "You mean me, right? You think *I* should calm down."

Not going to happen. Ian couldn't remember the last time he'd felt calm. The word sounded almost foreign on his tongue. *Stressed* had become his default state a long, long time ago. And they were talking about his girls. His precious, perfect twins—the sole reason he still managed to get out of bed in the mornings.

"We're just trying to help." Marianne smiled at him again, but the look in her eyes told another story. They glittered with pity.

Ian looked away. He neither needed nor wanted

pity—not for himself and definitely not for his daughters.

They were his tiny fighters—strong, sweet and resilient. Were they perfect? Of course not. What child was? But he would never want them to be anything but themselves—and to hell with anyone who had a problem with that.

Ian aimed his gaze back at the day care center director. "I appreciate your concern, but you're way off base. There's nothing wrong with Annie that a little patience and understanding won't cure. But perhaps I was foolish to think she could find that at Spring Forest Day School."

Then he spun on his heel to leave, because he'd said his piece. He was finished here.

Maybe his girls were too.

Rachel Gray lingered outside her boss's office at Spring Forest Day School, gripping a plastic tub of building blocks and trying to decide if she should walk inside or make herself scarce.

When Rachel had gotten word that Marianne wanted to see her in her office, she'd assumed it had something to do with her employment paperwork. She'd been so nervous at that idea that she'd forgotten to put down the toys she'd been organizing before she'd been summoned. Now here she was, clutching the box of blocks like it was a security blanket.

But maybe this impromptu meeting wasn't about her job application or her I-9 form. Just this morning, Rachel had mentioned that Annie Parsons seemed even more withdrawn and quiet than usual, and now Marianne seemed to be deep in conversation with the little girl's father. Did she want Rachel to join in the conversation so she could back her up?

No. Rachel turned to go. *No way.*

She'd been on the job for all of two weeks, and she was just a teacher's aide. She definitely wasn't ready to deal with an upset father. Just the thought of it made her stomach hurt.

But before Rachel could make her getaway, Ian Parsons came storming out of Marianne's office and plowed into the corner of the plastic tub in Rachel's hands. The bin wobbled, and she tried her best to keep it upright, but it did a somersault in the air, sending little wooden building blocks scattering far and wide. An avalanche of ABCs.

"Oh my gosh." Rachel's hand flew to her throat as Ian Parson's face turned as red as the shiny apple that little Johnny Cooper had brought her this morning. "I'm so sorry."

She dropped to her knees and began gathering as many blocks as she could into her arms, hating the way that her heart felt like it might pound right out of her chest.

He's a total stranger. And you're in a public place. He can't hurt you.

Ian sighed as he loomed above her, six feet two inches of pure fury and frustration. "Here, let me help."

Rachel shook her head. "No, really. It was my fault."

But he was already crouching beside her, picking up blocks and tossing them into the bin. Rachel would have gladly done it herself if he'd just go away and leave her alone.

No such luck, apparently.

"I suppose you heard what just went on in there," he said, jerking his head toward Marianne's office.

Rachel couldn't help but notice that some of the bite had gone out of his tone. She looked up to meet his gaze.

"I wasn't trying to eavesdrop." She swallowed hard. He had the most unusual eyes she'd ever seen up close before—light brown with flecks of gold. Warm, like amber honey.

Rachel might even have considered him handsome, if not for the angry vein throbbing in his forehead.

"It was probably hard not to overhear." The corner of his mouth hitched up a barely noticeable amount.

"Well, you were rather—" Rachel cleared her throat "—passionate."

That sounded better than *defensive* and *indignant*, didn't it?

Rachel didn't know why she was trying to sugar-coat things. She didn't like people who threw their weight around and raised their voices. Men, in particular.

But then Ian Parsons's hands slowed until he stopped moving altogether and just sat staring down at the blocks cradled in his palm. Two red *A*s were etched on their smooth wooden surfaces.

Annie and Abby.

He swallowed, and Rachel traced the movement up and down the muscular column of this throat. The fight seemed to drain slowly out of him, leaving something else in its place. Something rawer, more vulnerable.

Rachel moved quietly, picking up blocks and setting them gently in the bin. Being beside Ian in this private moment of reflection somehow felt more intrusive than standing outside Marianne's door listening to him argue with her boss.

Once the rest of the mess was cleaned up, she waited a beat and then gently pried the two *A* blocks from his grip. A lump formed in her throat for some ridiculous reason.

Ian's gaze lingered on the place where her fingertips had just brushed his skin, a slight furrow in his brow. Then he blinked hard, picked up the plastic tub full of blocks and stood.

Rachel scrambled to her feet and held out her hands, but he seemed to have no intention of handing over the bin.

"I've never seen you here before," he said.

"I'm new." She crossed her arms at her waist. Why couldn't she seem to figure out what to do with her hands? "My name is Rachel Gray. I started working here as a teaching assistant with the preschoolers a couple weeks ago."

"Do you know my daughters?" His amber eyes seemed to bore into her, making her head spin. "Abby and Annie Parsons? They're in the preschool class. Identical twins with blond pigtails that are usually lopsided."

Rachel felt herself smile. "Yes, I know Abby and Annie."

"So, what do you think?"

"About the pigtails?" She let out a little laugh. "Adorable."

He gave her another near-invisible half grin. If Rachel hadn't been looking at his mouth, she would have missed it entirely.

Why *was* she looking at his mouth?

"No, not the pigtails. I meant what do you think about their behavior? Do you agree with the day care director?" he asked.

The sudden arch of his eyebrow felt like a challenge.

Uh-oh.

The last thing Rachel wanted to do was to insert herself in an argument that had nothing to do with her, particularly after he'd just stormed out of Marianne's office and nearly reduced her to toddler road-kill. But he seemed to have calmed down a bit. When he'd been staring down at those twin *A* blocks in his hand, sadness had seemed to roll off him in waves.

He was asking for her opinion, plain and simple. What kind of child behavior specialist would she be if she didn't try and help? Not that he knew she was a child behavioral specialist, but still…

"To be honest, I understand where Marianne is coming from. While I don't necessarily agree that Annie should be removed from the classroom, I've noticed some developmental regression that concerns me." She paused to take a breath. Any hint of a smile on Ian Parsons's mouth had vanished completely. "Most of it appears to be self-soothing behaviors, things like rocking back and forth during story time and occasionally sucking her thumb.

Some kids simply grow out of this sort of thing, but others don't."

"And you think Annie falls into the latter group," Ian said tersely.

Rachel forced herself to square her shoulders and meet his gaze head-on. "I didn't say that."

"But you thought it."

She took a deep breath. "Mr. Parsons, it doesn't matter what I think. What matters is what we do about it."

We.

Rachel had said *we,* as if she, her boss and this impatient, seething man were some sort of team, which they clearly weren't. And that was fine. She wasn't sure she wanted to be part of a team that would have Ian Parsons as a member.

But she cared about his daughter, whether he believed that to be true or not. So she kept on talking, even if it suddenly felt like she was addressing a brick wall.

A brick wall with lovely, moody eyes and a startlingly chiseled jawline, but a brick wall nonetheless.

Stop noticing his looks. His runner's build and his unreasonably grumpy streak are his wife's problems, not yours.

"There are ways to help Annie come out of her shell and give her strategies to deal with whatever situations might be troubling her and causing these changes in her behavior. I've worked with children who are struggling in this way before." She lifted her chin. "I think I can help."

He gazed coolly at her, clearly unconvinced. "Do you, now?"

"I do," she said, holding out her arms once again so he could hand off the plastic tub. And maybe just a little bit of the burden that he was either unwilling or unable to accept.

He gave up the plastic tub but offered no indication whatsoever that he took her offer seriously.

Rachel should've felt relieved, but an irrational stab of disappointment hit her square in the feels.

What was she doing? She'd come to Spring Forest in search of peace and quiet. A nice, normal life. A *safe* life. And here she was, practically inviting herself into the den of yet another lion.

But the lion had other ideas.

"With all due respect, I think I know my daughters and 'whatever situations might be troubling' them better than you do," he said through gritted teeth.

He didn't make those irritating little air quotes around the words he'd parroted back to her, but he didn't have to. They swam before her eyes anyway, mocking her.

"Have a nice day, Miss Gray," he said, and then

he prowled off someplace else, leaving Rachel almost wishing that she'd overturned the box of blocks again, this time over his stubborn, annoying head.

Chapter Two

Ian's fantasy of taking the girls for a ride on their tricycles and then dining on dinosaur-shaped cuisine withered and died the second he turned his minivan into his shady cul-de-sac on Kingdom Creek Circle.

Elma's familiar sedan sat in his driveway, because of course it did. And he didn't spot anyone sitting inside the vehicle, which meant she'd used her emergency key for what was clearly a *non*emergency purpose. *Oh joy.*

He pulled the van alongside his mother-in-law's car, shifted into Park and somehow resisted the urge to bang his head against the steering wheel.

"Gammy here," Abby said, pointing at Elma's car and kicking her feet against her car seat.

"That's right. Aren't we lucky?" Ian glanced at the rearview mirror, gaze shifting toward Annie. "Isn't that right, sweetheart?"

Her eyes met his, and she gave him a tiny smile but said nothing.

Ian's heart sank to his shoes as he climbed out of the van—and he mentally berated himself for reacting this way just because of some rambling from an overreacting administrator. Was this how it was going to be now? He was going to analyze every tiny thing his daughters did or said?

No. He jerked the door to the back seat open. No, he wasn't going to do that. Abby and Annie were perfectly fine, just as he'd told Marianne and that nosy teacher's aide, Rachel Greene.

Wait, it was Gray, not Greene. Wasn't it? Rachel Greene was a character from *Friends*. Rachel Gray was a perfectly nonfictional thorn in his side.

"Gam-my, Gam-my," Abby sang in a sweet singsong voice as he unbuckled her car seat. Again, Ian snuck a hopeful glance at her twin, but Annie didn't join in.

Guilt nagged at him as he scooped the child into his arms and kissed the top of her head. "It's okay, sweetheart. Still waters run deep and all that."

Annie blinked her big blue eyes up at him, forehead scrunching, while Abby charged ahead, bolting for the door to the house.

"You're okay," he said quietly, giving Annie a squeeze. "*We're* okay."

But the doubt that crept into his tone was clearly discernible, even to his own ears, and he hated himself for it.

"I've made a tuna casserole, chicken tetrazzini and baked ziti." Elma greeted Ian in the foyer with a trio of covered dishes the minute he opened the door. "Which one do you want tonight? I can put the others in the refrigerator for later this week."

"Gammy!" Abby wrapped herself around one of Elma's legs.

Elma beamed. "Hi there, my sweet Abby. Yes, Gammy's here."

Ian put Annie down so he could gather the food and take it into the kitchen. He couldn't help noticing that Annie's greeting for her grandmother was far less effusive.

"What's that?" Elma cupped a hand to her ear. "Did you say you wanted me to stay for dinner?"

Annie hadn't said anything of the sort. In fact, she hadn't uttered a single word since he'd charged into the twins' classroom at Spring Forest Day School after his awkward conversation with Rachel Gray, pasted a smile on his face and taken them home.

Annie's silence felt palpable now, in a way that

it hadn't before. He found himself struggling to remember if pickup time was always like this and he just hadn't noticed. Abby was a chatterbox, always had been. Was it possible that her constant stream of babble had drowned out everything else, keeping him from noticing a real problem?

"Stay, Gammy! Stay!" Abby jumped up and down, pigtails bouncing.

Annie at last joined in the celebration, albeit more quietly. She and Abby clasped hands and began running circles around Elma, who looked as pleased as punch.

Ian's mother-in-law grinned in triumph. "The girls want me to stay. Shall I?"

What choice did he have?

"Of course, Elma. We'd be very happy if you joined us for dinner." He swallowed a sigh and headed toward the kitchen, arms weighed down with any and all manner of casseroles.

I've got to get that emergency key back.

"I'll set the table," Elma said as she swished past him toward the formal dining room.

Ian and the girls never ate in that room when it was just the three of them. He hadn't possessed strong feelings about the polished mahogany table when Serena picked it out at one of the antique shops up in Raleigh shortly after they'd bought the home in Kingdom Creek. But ever since he'd seen it covered from end to end in dishes the neighbors had brought by after his wife's funeral, he couldn't stand the sight of it—just like he could no longer stomach potato casserole.

Funeral potatoes, everyone called them in the South. He'd loved them as a kid. Never again.

He plopped the pans of food down onto the counter.

"The girls are off washing their hands. I taught them how, you know. They just love that little giraffe-shaped stepping stool I bought for the bathroom," Elma said as she breezed into the room. She looked him up and down. "You seem awfully tired, Ian."

You don't know the half of it.

"Shall I stay after dinner and give the girls their baths so you can get some rest?" Elma said, reaching into one of the cabinets for two china plates, along with the *Angelina Ballerina* plastic dishes that Abby and Annie preferred. They loved the *Angelina Ballerina* picture books, which chronicled the life of a dancing mouse. Ian had read them aloud to the girls so many times that he could probably recite them in his sleep.

He focused on the plate with the pirouetting mouse and her pink tutu so he wouldn't have to meet Elma's gaze. "I can handle bath time."

"Are you sure? I really don't mind."

Ian's temples throbbed. He felt for Elma. He really did. Serena had been an only child, her parents' pride and joy. Her father had passed away back when Serena was in college at Wake Forest. After that, Serena had been Elma's whole world.

And then the twins had been born. Elma had doted on them from the very beginning, but now she seemed to be holding on to them more and more. Intellectually, Ian knew it was simply her way of dealing with losing her cherished daughter.

But it was hard to not take her interference personally—as if she didn't trust him to be able to look after his daughters himself. His sensitivity on that point was all the stronger because…well…he had a few doubts of his own. No matter how hard he tried, Ian couldn't help feeling that he wasn't enough for his girls. Serena had always been the better half of their whole. He was well aware of his own short-comings, without Elma's constant reminders that he didn't quite know what he was doing. Every now and then, he honestly suspected that she wanted to take them away from him, that Elma secretly thought the girls would be better off living with their grand-mother instead of their father. Sometimes, in his darker moments, Ian even agreed.

Times like today, for instance.

"I said I'll handle bath time," he repeated—his voice a little too gruff. A little too loud.

Elma bristled. Ian slumped.

He really needed to stop lashing out at people like that. Serena would have been horrified if she'd seen him at the school today. Ian never used to speak to anyone disrespectfully. But lately, it had been getting harder and harder to hold on to his temper when he had to deal with life's little hiccups. Ian's mom was recovering from knee surgery down in Florida, where his folks had retired. He didn't dare burden them with something like this. He already felt like he was disappointing people at every turn—not just Elma, but Annie and Abby too. Even Serena. When something big came along, like Annie possibly getting tossed out of preschool, it was just too much.

You don't have to do it alone, you know. Someone just tried to help you.

Rachel Gray had looked him square in the eyes and offered him the most elusive thing of all—hope. And Ian had all but laughed in her face.

Beside him, Elma folded and refolded a dish towel. No doubt she was currently making a mental list of all the ways he could screw up a bubble bath.

"Sorry," he said quietly. "It's just been a long day, but I'm looking forward to getting the girls bathed and ready for bed. Maybe another time."

"I understand," Elma said in a tone that indicated she didn't understand in the slightest. "We should probably get whatever casserole you choose into the oven. I'm sure the twins are hungry."

She reached around him to preheat the oven. "The tuna has the most protein, but I know the twins have probably had fish sticks a few times this week already."

Accurate. Why did that suddenly feel like a crime?

"They *love* the tetrazzini," Elma said, puffing out her chest a little.

Ian hated chicken tetrazzini, and while the twins did indeed love it, they made a huge mess every time it was on the menu—a mess that migrated from the plate to their faces, their hair, their clothes, their seats, the table, the floor and occasionally even the ceiling. Ian wasn't sure he had it in him to pick up a mountain of discarded noodles tonight. Come to think of it, he was sure he didn't.

But he'd already laid down the law about bath time. Experience had taught him to pick and choose his battles where Elma was concerned.

"Chicken tetrazzini, it is." He smiled, but his heart wasn't in it.

As he shoved the casserole dish into the oven, he couldn't help but wonder what Rachel Gray was having for dinner. He wasn't sure why, but he had a feeling she would love dinosaur-shaped chicken nuggets…

So long as she wouldn't be forced to eat them with Ian sitting beside her. And for that, he had no one but himself to blame.

* * *

Rachel yawned as she pedaled her vintage cruiser bicycle toward Spring Forest Day School the following morning. Thank goodness the preschool was within biking distance of the residence hotel where she was currently staying near the center of town. There was zero room in her budget for a car, and so far, her modest pay at Spring Forest Day hadn't afforded her the means to move from the residence hotel to an actual cottage or even an apartment.

Not that she was complaining. She loved her new life in Spring Forest. Compared to her old life in Virginia, things in North Carolina were a cakewalk.

But this morning, she admittedly wasn't at her best. She'd barely slept a wink last night, and on the few occasions she'd managed to drift off, Ian Parsons kept turning up in her dreams. Broody. Melancholy. Intimidating. And far, *far* too handsome.

Rachel climbed off her bike and wove a chain lock through the powder blue metal and the bike rack near the entrance to the school. She couldn't imagine her bike getting stolen anywhere in this quaint small town, but she'd made the mistake of being too naive and trusting before. Experience had taught her to err on the side of caution. Which was probably why alarm bells started ringing in the back of her head the moment she turned around and saw none other than Ian walking toward her, flanked on either side by his sweet twins.

There was nothing at all outwardly threatening about his appearance. He was dressed in a freshly pressed business suit with a crisp white shirt and a silk tie that looked like it had come in a bright orange shopping bag with the word *Hermès* stamped on the side. But his slightly mussed hair and a missed spot of shaving cream near the corner of his jaw gave him a relatable, boy-next-door vibe that made her heart do a little flip.

Or maybe that had more to do with the sight of Annie and Abby, who each clutched one of Ian's big hands while at the same time juggling modest bouquets of wildflowers that looked handpicked. They wore matching floral dresses with sweet Peter Pan collars. As usual, their pigtails were slightly askew.

The girls were beyond precious. Anyone's heart would skip a beat at the sight of them. Ian was merely an accessory.

Keep telling yourself that.

Rachel did an about-face, cheeks going warm as she fumbled unnecessarily with her bike lock. Maybe if she stalled long enough, she could avoid another run-in with the school's crankiest dad. It wasn't out of the realm of possibility, was it? Until yesterday, she'd successfully avoided any and all interaction with the man.

But within seconds, a throat cleared behind her. A distinctly *masculine*-sounding throat, followed by a gravelly voice that seemed to tickle her insides. "Good morning, Miss Gray."

So much for trying to make herself invisible. It had worked for the character in *The Invisible Boy*, a picture book that the kids in her class always enjoyed at story hour. Harder to swing for a nonfictional teacher's aide, apparently.

She spun around, shoulders squared. The girls were gone. It was just him, his fancy tie, the cute little dab of shaving cream and the two bouquets of wildflowers—one in each hand. He looked like he'd just walked off the set of a Hallmark cards commercial.

"Good morning, Mr. Parsons," she said as coldly as she could manage. "I, um, didn't see you there."

He tilted his head. "Really? Not even when you looked straight at me and then turned around to secure your bicycle?" He shot a dubious glance at the lock. "For a second time."

Busted.

"Can't be too careful," she said, trying her best to focus on his tie or the brightly colored flowers he was holding. Anything to keep from looking into those piercing amber eyes of his.

"'Careful'?" Ian arched a brow. "Is that what we're calling it?"

"Yes," Rachel said primly.

What was wrong with being careful? She'd made enough mistakes for a lifetime already. *Careful* was her new favorite word.

"I thought perhaps you were trying to avoid me," Ian said, shrugging a single muscular shoulder. "Not that I would blame you."

His candor caught Rachel by surprise. She wasn't sure what to say. She didn't want to let him off the hook by pretending she hadn't been rattled by their exchange the previous day, nor did she want to re-ignite their awkward conversation from then. In a matter of minutes, she'd watched his mood change on a dime. Twice. She knew better than to trust this new, charming version of Ian Parsons.

Oh, so now you think the cranky dad is charming?

"These are for you." He thrust one of the bouquets toward her. "I know they're nothing fancy. The girls helped me pick them this morning."

Rachel melted a little bit inside, despite every effort not to. She couldn't quite help it. Ian Parsons and his twins picking wildflowers before school was a mental picture that was far too adorable to resist.

"Thank you. They're lovely." She took the bouquet, and instantly, the sweet scent of pink mountain garland and purple rocket larkspur wrapped her in a heady, fragrant cloud.

Rachel tried to remember the last time anyone had given her flowers.

Had anyone given her flowers before?

"The other bouquet is for your boss." Ian sighed. "I'm not sure flowers are going to be enough to convince her not to kick Annie out of school, but it's worth a shot."

"I'm sure Marianne will love them," Rachel said, trying to sidestep the mention of Annie's possible expulsion.

It's not your business, remember? Ian had made that clear already.

But then he turned his honey-colored eyes toward her, and his expression grew softer, less guarded. "Yesterday you said you thought you could help Annie?"

It sounded more like a question than a statement of fact, and Rachel knew that this was the moment to simply shake her head and walk away. But she couldn't. Not when there was a child in need—a child she could help. It just wasn't in her DNA.

"I did, yes. I'm just wondering if we're on the same page, though. Yesterday, you—"

"Yesterday, I was being an idiot," he said, finishing the thought for her. "And then last night, we went home and I was suddenly aware that Annie hardly made a peep all night."

Rachel wished this information came as a surprise, but it didn't.

"I can't believe I haven't noticed it before. Abby has always been the more outgoing one, but Annie seems to be all but disappearing in her sister's shadow. They like to play a game where they pretend to be their favorite animals. They've been playing the game so long that I can't even remember when it started. Abby is always a cat and Annie's a dog. But last night, I noticed that Annie's not even barking anymore. That's bad, isn't it? Toddlers should talk. Dogs should definitely bark." His gaze flitted over her shoulder, and his brow furrowed.

Rachel turned to see what had captured his attention and spotted one of the flyers she'd seen plastered all over town. The orange face of Oliver, a cat who'd apparently gone missing, gazed back at her. He seemed like the sort of cat who definitely had opinions about barking dogs.

She swiveled to face Annie and Abby's father again. "Mr. Parsons, it sounds like you're starting to notice the same things I've observed in the classroom. And while it's something to be concerned about, I can assure you it's not the end of the world. This sort of thing happens a lot with twins. Sometimes, one twin will do all the talking, all the socializing, and the shier twin will just let them—

particularly if the quieter twin is struggling emotionally."

He nodded. "I think that might be exactly what's going on. You're *sure* it's not the end of the world? There's some way to fix this that *doesn't* involve taking Annie out of school and away from her sister? Because I promise you, if Abby and Annie are separated, it will be the end of the world. For both of them."

Rachel nodded. "I understand, but I think some one-on-one time with Annie outside of the classroom would get her where she needs to be. Right now, she's letting Abby do everything for her. Maybe I could give you some exercises that you and your wife could do at home with Annie?"

His expression sobered and he let out a ragged breath. "Wow, you really are new in town, aren't you?"

Rachel blinked. "I'm not following."

"My wife passed away. It's just me and the girls now," he said.

"Oh." Rachel's throat clogged. Why hadn't she guessed this was what was going on? His comment about lopsided pigtails had been a major clue, as had the way Annie—and Abby, in a different way— seemed to be struggling. "I'm so sorry to hear that."

"Thank you, but honestly, I don't need your sympathy, Miss Gray. What I need is some help for my daughter."

She bit down on her lip, doing her best to tamp down any sorrow that might creep into her features, but she knew the effort was probably futile. Rachel had lost her own mom when she was just a baby. Her heart went out to Abby and Annie more than he could possibly know.

"Can you do that for me? I can compensate you generously." Ian tilted his head, and she caught another glimpse of the shaving cream that clung to his jaw. The urge to reach out and brush it away with the pad of her thumb was almost irresistible. "Can you help us?"

Tell him no. This has disaster written all over it. For once, you need to put yourself first instead of getting involved in someone else's problems. Now, more than ever, you have to look after yourself.

Rachel felt herself smile as the petals on the flowers in her hand fluttered in the gentle Carolina breeze.

"Yes, of course I'll help."

Chapter Three

Ian's doorbell rang at exactly six thirty that evening—the appointed time for Rachel's visit. He'd had just enough time to pick the twins up from school, get them bathed and changed and order a pizza before he loosened his tie and made his way to the door.

This was a meeting, obviously. An *important* meeting. But they still had to eat, and so did Rachel. Ian assumed she did, anyway.

He'd forgotten what life without kids was like. Rachel probably didn't normally have to juggle dinner with trying to simultaneously wrangle twin toddlers. She might have had time after work to sit down and enjoy a peaceful meal already.

Why are you suddenly obsessing about Rachel Gray's eating habits?

Ian blew out a breath. He was nervous, and he wasn't sure why.

Because he was worried about Annie, obviously. That was the only possible explanation. Why else would his blood be pumping so fast and hard through his veins?

He swung the door open, and the disappointment that coursed through him at the sight of Elma standing on his porch made him think that perhaps his nerves weren't entirely toddler related, after all.

"Elma. You brought dinner." His gaze dropped to the casserole dish in her hands and he sighed. "Again."

"I sure did. I don't mind helping out. Honest, I don't. I know how much you have on your plate, and you'll notice that I didn't use my key." Was it his imagination, or was her smile slightly frosty around the edges? "As you requested, I knocked on the front door like a common stranger."

Definitely not his imagination, then.

Maybe he shouldn't have said anything to her about the key. But after choking down a plateful of chicken tetrazzini against his will and fighting for the right to make even the smallest decisions about his own children's bedtime routine, he'd finally caved and asked her to stop letting herself into the house. At least, he'd stopped short of asking for the key back altogether.

"You'll never be a stranger around here, Elma," he said, opening the door wide.

Tears filled her eyes as she breezed past him. "Well, it worries me, you know. Grandparents have zero legal rights. Did you know that? Absolutely none. You could pack up Abby and Annie and move clear across the country if you wanted to. Across the *world*, even. And I wouldn't be able to do a thing about it. What would happen to me? You and the twins are the only family I have left, Ian. You probably haven't thought much about that."

Ian had indeed thought about it. It was hard not to when Elma reminded him of this fact every other day.

"No one is moving, Elma. You have my word." He definitely shouldn't have mentioned the key. Oh, if only he could go back in time and stop the words from tumbling out of his mouth. Yesterday had been an epic fail on numerous fronts.

"Well, that's good to hear. Serena wouldn't want—" Elma's voice came to an abrupt halt as her gaze drifted over Ian's shoulder. "Hello, there. Can we help you with something?"

Ian turned to find Rachel walking up the front path. A forbidden zing coursed through him when he noticed that two of the wildflowers from the bouquet he and the girls had given her were tucked into her hair. Lush auburn waves fell around her shoulders, perfectly offset by the two small daisies pinned just above her right ear. She almost looked like one of the Disney princesses that Abby and Annie loved so much.

"Hi." She aimed a tentative glance at Ian. "Is this still a good time for our appointment?"

Appointment. It was a benign word, perfectly harmless. But the way Elma drew back her head and widened her eyes, any casual bystander would have thought she'd called it a "date." Or maybe a "torrid affair."

"I didn't realize you had plans this evening," Elma said, and then under her breath, she added, "Although I suppose now I understand the business about the key..."

Rachel's pretty pink mouth curved into a frown. Why, oh why, had he noticed her chosen shade of lipstick? Sweet and fairy-light, the exact color of a pink carnation. "Key?" she asked.

Say something.

The evening was already turning into a disaster, and she hadn't even made it off the welcome mat yet.

"Rachel, please come in. The girls will be thrilled to see you." Ian waved her inside as Elma glared at him with renewed horror, clearly appalled that he would introduce his date to his daughters.

Not that this was anything remotely resembling a date, but still. Would it really be so terrible if he wanted to date someone? Was he supposed to turn into a monk now that he was a widower?

He glanced at Elma. *Yes. Yes, you are*, her eyes seemed to scream.

"Elma, this is Rachel Gray. She works at Abby and Annie's preschool, and she's here this evening to do some extra work with the girls." Ian's attention swiveled between the two women. "Rachel, this is the twins' grandmother, Elma Miller."

Rachel smiled and held out her hand. "Oh, it's so lovely to meet you, Mrs. Miller."

Elma gave her hand as brief a shake as was possible while she looked her up and down. "You're a teacher at the preschool?"

Rachel shrugged one slender shoulder. "A teacher's aide, actually. I don't know if Mr. Parsons has mentioned it to you or not, but Annie's struggling a bit at school and I think I might be able to help."

"Oh." The set of Elma's shoulders relaxed ever so slightly. "Okay, then. I hope you're hungry. I made enchiladas."

"Actually, I ordered pizza a few minutes ago, Elma," Ian said as a pizza delivery car pulled up to the curb.

He couldn't remember the last time his home had been the epicenter of this much activity. His head was starting to hurt. Ian had forgotten how much energy it took to have an actual, real life.

Elma raised her eyebrows in Rachel's direction. A silent question.

"Enchiladas sound lovely," Rachel said. "Why don't we have both?"

Smart girl.

Why did Ian have a feeling she was the exact right person to help him deal with Annie and Abby? Maybe even Elma, as well.

"Olé," Ian said.

"Bellissimo," Rachel said, and then their eyes met and held for the briefest of moments.

Just long enough for Ian to feel the tiniest spark of…something. It had been so long since he'd experienced anything like the sensation that he couldn't even put a label on it.

Then Rachel cleared her throat and looked away, and Ian remembered that he was a widowed father. With twins. And a busybody mother-in-law who was watching him like a hawk at the moment, with an expression on her face that said she hoped he choked on an enchilada so she could raise Abby and Annie as her own.

Elma glanced back and forth between Ian and Rachel, brow furrowing, and then marched off toward the kitchen with her tray of enchiladas. Ian turned toward Rachel and mouthed *I'm sorry* behind his mother-in-law's back. He hadn't planned on Elma's presence this evening.

Then again, when had that ever stopped her from barging right in?

Rachel's forehead crinkled, as if she had no idea what he might be apologizing for. An hour later, when the five of them were seated in the dining room, she probably had a better idea.

"I'm just not sure how I feel about a stranger coming into the house and spending time around my grandchildren," Elma said, eyeing Rachel from across the table.

Rachel was flanked on either side by the twins, who'd both insisted on sitting beside her. They were so captivated by the sight of one of their teachers outside the walls of their school—and in their very own home, no less—that they could barely concentrate on the food in front of them.

"Rachel, er, Miss Gray isn't a stranger. She sees Annie and Abby every day at Spring Forest Day School."

Elma huffed. For a minute, Ian thought she was going to launch into another one of her diatribes about how toddlers were too young to be spending all day at school, but thankfully, she refrained.

"And you're an aide, is that right?" Elma said, narrowing her gaze.

Rachel put down her slice of pizza and wiped her

fingertips on the napkin in her lap. "Yes, I am. But it might make you feel more comfortable to know that before I moved here, I was working as an accredited child behavior specialist in Virginia. I'm currently waiting for my state credentials to be approved so I can work in the North Carolina school system."

Ian hadn't been privy to this information, but it certainly explained a lot.

"The job at the day care is the first one I found." Rachel shrugged one shoulder. "It will do for now."

"Miss Rachel my friend," Abby said, gazing at Rachel with stars in her eyes.

Ian's gaze darted to Annie. In the not-so-distant past, she would have echoed the sentiment. Now she simply sat staring quietly at her plate.

"That's right, sweetheart," he said as his throat went thick. "She's a friend to you and your sister both."

That seemed to settle the matter with Elma, at least for the time being. Once dinner was over and the dishes were all cleaned and put away, she made herself scarce. Ian could breathe a sigh of relief.

For now, at least.

"I'm sorry about Elma."

It was the first thing Ian said as he descended the stairs after tucking Annie and Abby in bed for the night. It was also the third time he'd apologized to her about his mother-in-law's overall demeanor.

Possibly even the fourth. Rachel had begun to lose count.

"It's fine. Truly." Rachel laughed under her breath.

She thought it best to try and stay quiet so the twins could fall asleep. But whispering felt intimate in a way that it probably shouldn't, so she cleared her throat and did her best to sound businesslike. Professional. After all, that was why she was here.

Right?

Most definitely, she told herself, even as her gaze strayed toward the sharp cut of Ian's jaw—the exact spot where she'd spied the small dab of shaving cream this morning. Her fingertips tingled, as if her ridiculous fantasy of brushing it away had been an actual flesh-and-blood memory and she could recall the sensation of his warm skin under her touch.

"How long ago did your wife pass away?" she heard herself say. The urge to immediately clamp her hand over her mouth was very potent and *very* real, but that didn't seem very professional, so she focused on backtracking instead. "I'm so sorry. I don't mean to pry. It just seems that Elma might be having a hard time adjusting to things."

Ian shook his head. "No need to apologize. You're absolutely right. She's definitely having a hard time. Just like Annie, I suppose."

Rachel nodded. "These things take time."

"It's been about a year," Ian said in a voice so low

and gravelly that a chill ran up and down Rachel's spine.

What was she doing here? This family needed space and time to heal. Maybe Elma was right. Rachel was an intruder, and her presence seemed to be causing more drama than actual help.

"You're great at this, you know," Ian said, tipping his head toward the twins' room at the top of the stairs. "The girls really respond to you. Abby seemed much calmer tonight."

Rachel breathed a tiny sigh of relief. Perhaps she wasn't as out of her element as she'd imagined. "When one twin acts out, it's usually to try and keep the parent's attention on them instead of the other twin. I think Abby probably senses that Annie wants to withdraw, so she's subconsciously doing her best to help make that happen."

A rare smile tugged at Ian's lips. "And you managed to get Annie out of her shell a bit after dinner."

Rachel nodded. "Consequently, Abby probably felt less compelled to keep all the attention on herself."

Once Elma had gone home, Ian, Rachel and the girls had spent some time in the twins' grand playroom. Located upstairs, just off their bedroom, the playroom featured everything a little girl could want—all in soft shades of blush pink and ivory. There were stuffed animals ranging from unicorns to stick horses to teddy bears to Minions, a table set for imaginary tea, a coloring station, a miniature kitchen and, in the center of it all, a gauzy pink play tent piled high with plush pillows and fuzzy blankets. Glow-in-the-dark stars lit up the ceiling, and a spinning lamp cast shadows of carousel horses gliding up and down the walls.

It was the loveliest room Rachel had ever seen. At first, Abby had been keen to show her around, chattering away, while Annie followed quietly on her heels. In an effort to draw Annie into the conversation, Rachel suggested the four of them play a game. She'd spied Candy Land, one of her own childhood favorites, tucked among the puzzles and storybooks on the polished white bookshelves that ran from one end of the room to the other. As Rachel, Ian, Annie and Abby moved their playing pieces from the Peppermint Forest, through the Lollipop Woods, toward the dreaded Molasses Swamp, Annie slowly began to relax. By the time Ian reached the Candy Castle and declared himself the victor, the sweet little girl had crawled into Rachel's lap.

"Don't give me all the credit. Annie's behavior after dinner tonight probably had more to do with you than you realize," she said, wanting to make sure Ian knew that he'd had just as much to do with the baby steps they'd accomplished tonight as Rachel had. Maybe even more so. "The best possible thing a parent can do to help a child overcome shyness is to show them how it's done. You're Annie's most important role model. When she sees you being open and friendly around others, Annie will feel more comfortable doing the same."

Ian drew in a breath and looked at her. Long and hard.

Had she overstepped? It was obvious that Ian didn't entertain much. Elma's surprised reaction when Rachel arrived had told her everything she needed to know about his social life. The man obviously didn't have one.

Not that Rachel was in a position to judge. She wasn't exactly a social butterfly herself...with good reason.

"What would it take for you to resign your position at the day care and work with Annie and Abby full-time?" Ian finally said.

Wait.

What?

Rachel wasn't sure what she'd expected him to say, but it definitely hadn't been that. "You, um, want me to quit my job?"

"I think Marianne might have been right. Spring Forest Day School isn't the best place for them—not right now. They need a break. The girls need one-on-one attention. They need to spend time with someone who understands what they're going through, someone with the skills to help them through it."

He gave her a look so intense that she almost forgot how to breathe. "Someone like you."

"But—" She shook her head. No way. She couldn't quit her job and work for Ian Parsons. That would make him her *boss*.

"Whatever they're paying you, I'll double it," he said. "Even if it's just until your state accreditation comes through."

Rachel laughed. "That's hilarious, but no."

"I wasn't joking," he said without cracking a smile.

Well then.

Her heart beat wildly in her chest. She wasn't seriously considering this, was she? Her job at the day care wasn't exactly the most challenging thing she'd ever done, and the pay was certainly nothing to write home about, but it was safe and consistent. It represented the thing Rachel wanted most in the world—security. She couldn't give that up to work under the sole authority of a temperamental man who might change his mind and dismiss her on a whim.

Double the money was tempting, though. That kind of cash would allow her to move out of the residence hotel and into somewhere nicer. It might even be enough to allow her to build up a little nest egg too.

And she loved his girls. That was an undeniable fact. They tugged on her heartstrings in a major way, now more than ever. Otherwise, she never would have agreed to come over this evening.

Rachel swallowed. "Can I ask you a question?"

"Sure." Ian crossed his arms, not exactly the picture of an open book.

She plowed forward anyway. "Why me?"

"Because, like I said, you're great at this. The girls obviously adore you, and you know how to get results. I could see a difference just from a couple of hours of you working with them. With you helping them, they'd probably be ready to go back into the classroom soon. I just know it. And..." He paused.

To Rachel's mortification, she realized she was hanging on his every word. "And?"

"And you clearly have no problem telling me when I'm doing something wrong." He laughed under his breath. "In a good way—a *constructive* way—rather than an Elma sort of way."

Her face went instantly hot. "I never said you were doing anything wrong."

"I'm pretty sure you implied I was a hermit." His expression turned uncharacteristically sheepish. "And you might be right. I've just never thought about what kind of example that was setting for my kids."

Rachel took a shaky inhale. Why did he have to be so soulful and introspective when she least expected it? It made him seem borderline charming, even. Just like this morning with the flowers. The colorful bouquet sat in a mason jar on the tiny table in her small room back at the residence hotel, a bright spot in the otherwise drab space. Every time she looked at it, she could feel a smile tug at her lips.

Which probably had a lot to do with the *yes* that was currently dancing on the tip of her tongue.

Could she really work for him, though?

"Where do you live?" Ian asked as though he could see straight into her head, where the image of the flowers blazed as brightly as a summer sunset. "I know you have your bike instead of a car. Would the commute be a problem for you to handle twice a day?"

It…might be. Compared to the school, his house was in the opposite direction from her hotel. A bike ride that long was manageable but not ideal. And it would really turn into a slog if there was bad weather. The few times it had rained since she'd started at the school, she'd gotten a ride from co-workers, but obviously, that wouldn't be an option if she was working for Ian.

"I'm just asking because I have an in-law suite downstairs," he continued. "It's got its own private entrance, so you can have your privacy. And honestly, if you stayed here, you'd be doing me a favor, as long as you didn't mind having your hours be a little flexible. If you were here with the girls, I wouldn't have to find a sitter or call Elma if I had to work late or leave early in the morning."

"I live at the residence hotel downtown. The in-law suite sounds…" Rachel swallowed. *Wonderful.* It sounded like a dream come true, actually. Who wouldn't rather live in the utopian neighborhood of Kingdom Creek instead of a cheap hotel? "…very generous. I couldn't possibly accept, though."

"What if I offered to *triple* your salary—plus free housing?" Ian said, grinning despite the fact that he was clearly trying to talk her into something she wasn't completely sold on.

She laughed. "I'd say you'd lost your mind."

"Then, you'd better say yes before I offer to qua-druple it." He shrugged.

This sort of intense negotiation probably should have made her uncomfortable. Why didn't it?

Because you already know you're going to say yes. It's an amazing opportunity. And more impor-tantly, you adore this man's children.

Emotions aside, taking the job was the smart thing to do…the logical thing. As long as she could remember that it was just temporary. She'd simply have to do her absolute best not to get too attached to the girls. Or Ian, for that matter. Otherwise, it would hurt terribly when it was time for her to leave. And of course, there was no telling how long she'd actu-ally be able to stay here.

At least, that's what Rachel told herself as she nodded and said, "Okay, then. My answer is yes, but it's just until my state accreditation comes through."

"We have a deal?" His grin was so boyish and genuine that Rachel's head spun a little.

Stop it. This is a simple business arrangement, nothing more.

Rachel nodded. "We do. A temporary deal."

But then they shook on it and a not-so-businesslike shiver coursed through her as Ian took her hand in his. She smiled and pretended not to notice, even as building blocks tumbled through her imagination, just like when they'd first met. Only this time, their letters spelled out an unmistakable message.

T-R-O-U-B-L-E.

Chapter Four

The following three days passed in a whirlwind. Rachel gave her notice at Spring Forest Day School the morning after Ian had offered her the job, and Marianne had graciously told her she was free to begin her nanny position after the end of the week.

Rachel was equal parts grateful and nervous. She was eager to start working with Abby and Annie, but if she was so easily disposable at the day care center, that probably meant she wouldn't be able to go crawling back if her new job ended up being a total disaster. She was about to jump right into the deep end.

Sink or swim.

The thought was daunting enough that she found herself holding her breath on Saturday morning as she stood on the path leading to the in-law suite at Ian's palatial home.

"Wow." Rachel felt her eyes go wide.

She tried to keep her mouth from dropping open at the sight of the cute little structure that stood just beyond the main house. With its buttercup-yellow shingles and gabled roof, it was more than a simple in-law suite. It was a full-on miniature version of the home where Ian and his daughters lived.

"It's a refurbished carriage house. And I promise it's not as fancy as it looks on the outside. The interior totals less than three hundred square feet. I think that makes it qualify as one of those tiny houses they're always talking about on HGTV," Ian said.

Rachel slid her gaze toward him. "Don't take this the wrong way, but I never would have pegged you as an HGTV fan."

He arched an eyebrow. "Do you watch it?"

"All the time." Rachel loved the house-hunting shows, especially the ones where people moved to other countries. It made her feel like fresh starts were not just possible but had the potential to be wonderful, even if her own new beginning hadn't been quite so glamorous.

Until now, anyway.

"Then, you understand the appeal," Ian said.

Of course she did. It was all about wish fulfill-
ment, which just went to show that you couldn't
judge a book by its cover. On the surface, Ian appeared to have everything anyone could possibly
want. But he still wished for things, just like she did.

Rachel wondered what those things might be, but
she didn't dare ask.

"Are you sure Elma is going to be okay with
this?" she said instead. Because something told her
that Ian's mother-in-law would sell her soul to live
on the same premises with her granddaughters.

"Don't worry about Elma," he said, but the set of
his jaw hardened a bit. Clearly, *someone* was worried about her.

But that was none of Rachel's business. She was
just an employee here, not a friend. And certainly
not family. The sooner she accepted that fact, the
better.

You cannot *get too attached to those girls.*

"Elma left yesterday for a trip with her antiques
club. They went to Asheville," Ian's forehead furrowed. "I suspect she might be trying to prove a
point to me about how badly we need her around
here."

Rachel's footsteps slowed. "You mean you haven't
told her you hired me?"

"Not yet. Once she comes back from her trip, I'm
going to take her to lunch and have a heart-to-heart

about the girls and what a benefit you'll be to them. It's going to be fine."

"Are you sure about that?"

"Absolutely." Ian gave a firm nod, and Rachel got the definite impression that the subject was closed.

Good. She had no desire to insert herself into anyone else's family drama. Just the thought of it made her stomach squirm.

"Well, here it is." Ian twisted the doorknob and pushed the door of the carriage house open. "Your new home sweet home."

Rachel hesitated on the top step of the private porch, where pots of hydrangeas in periwinkle blue and soft, cotton candy pink flanked either side of the entrance to her new carriage house home. "Um…"

Ian raked a hand through his hair and glanced inside the building. White eyelet curtains fluttered in the breeze and the pine floors were so smooth and polished that they shone like a mirror. "It's too small, isn't it?"

Rachel shook her head. "Goodness, no. It's at least twice as big as my room back at the hotel." The house was a dream come true, more perfect than she'd dared to imagine.

She swallowed hard. "I'm just wondering if the door has a lock."

He'd walked right in without a key or anything. Granted, the sweet little building was tucked behind the main house, hidden from view, but Rachel couldn't stay in a place without a lock on the door. Even with a dead bolt and a chain, she'd shoved a chair in front of the door every night in her hotel room when she went to bed.

"Oh." Ian nodded. "Of course. I just usually don't keep it locked. The neighborhood is gated, so I guess I'm not always as careful as I should be."

"If you could find a key for me, I'd appreciate it. It's just a habit for me to make sure my place is always locked up tight," Rachel said. A blatant lie. "Safety first and all that."

"Sure. I get it," he said, although there was no real way he understood. How could he possibly? "Let me show you around, and then I'll run to the house and get you a set of keys."

"Great. Thanks."

He probably thought she was completely paranoid. If he did, though, he didn't let it show. He seemed as relaxed as she'd ever seen him as he walked her through the interior of the carriage house.

It had an open floor plan, giving the space a cozy, charming feel. And to Rachel's great relief, it was fully, if simply, furnished. The sofa was covered in blue-and-white gingham fabric that matched the slip covers on the two dining chairs that were tucked under a small café table in the breakfast nook. The bedroom was decorated in various shades of white and ivory, with a pretty brass headboard and a small bouquet of daisies on the nightstand in a blue toile vase. The vase looked like it might be an antique, a far cry from the mason jar that had held her wildflower arrangement back in her hotel room.

"The girls insisted on getting flowers for you at the market this morning. They're really excited you're here… We all are." Ian cleared his throat. "I mean, I'm sure the three of you will get along great."

Butterflies swarmed in Rachel's belly. This was all too much—the outlandish salary, the adorable living quarters and *more* flowers. She wasn't accustomed to being treated like this. If she wasn't careful, she might get used to it.

Don't. You never know when you might have to pick up and move.

In truth, Rachel had no idea how long she might be able to stay here. It could be a week, a month… maybe even just a day. Putting down roots just wasn't possible.

No matter how appealing those roots might be.

"I should probably start getting my things." She tipped her head in the direction of the front yard, where her Uber driver was still parked at the curb.

She didn't have much to unpack. Her bicycle, her boxes of books and the contents of the blue leather suitcase her grandmother had given her for her high school graduation made up the bulk of her possessions—and the suitcase wasn't even full. But showing up on a bike with her suitcase wedged between the handlebars hadn't seemed like the way to go. Thank goodness an Uber from downtown Spring Forest to Kingdom Creek had cost under ten dollars.

Ian blinked. "I didn't see a truck or anything. I guess I thought your moving boxes were coming later."

"I don't have much. No truck necessary." Nervous laughter bubbled up Rachel's throat.

She was a grown, professional woman. She should have had more to show for her twenty-eight years on God's green earth than a newly refurbished bicycle and a beat-up suitcase and a couple boxes of books.

Ian didn't pry, thankfully. Rachel wasn't sure how she would have explained the situation if he had.

She let out a shaky exhale. He'd been right about the dimensions of the carriage house. Her cottage was perfect, but it was on the small side—especially the bedroom. Especially when she had company in that bedroom. With his broad shoulders and masculine frame, Ian seemed to be taking up all the air. Why else would she feel so breathless all of a sudden?

"I'll give you a hand," he said.

"You really don't have to." He'd done so much for her already, and he was her boss. She couldn't possibly let him help her move.

"I insist," he countered, and before she could issue another objection, he strode past her, heading in the direction of the front drive and her Uber driver's car with everything she owned tucked neatly into the trunk, with room to spare.

Okay, then.

Rachel squared her shoulders and followed. The more time she spent with Ian, the more she was beginning to realize that he was a man who didn't often take no for an answer. Yet another reason this entire arrangement needed to be temporary.

Ian hauled Rachel's robin's egg–blue cruiser bicycle out of the trunk of her Uber driver's car and set it down on the pavement. The only other items in the sedan's trunk were an ancient-looking suitcase and two small cardboard boxes.

This couldn't be everything. Clearly, Rachel had left most of her things back at the residence hotel. Maybe she'd been embarrassed to admit that she hadn't been able to arrange for everything at once.

He reached into the trunk for the suitcase, but she beat him to it, grabbing it by the handle and heaving it toward the lawn. The battered thing didn't even have wheels. Ian gathered the remaining boxes and set them down beside the bike as the driver pulled away from the curb. No wonder Rachel hadn't managed to get any more of her belongings to his house. The driver didn't seem helpful in the slightest.

"I can give you a ride back to the hotel for the rest of your things, if you like," Ian said.

He'd already made a similar offer the other day after they'd settled on the terms of her employment, but Rachel had insisted on taking care of the logistics of her move by herself. Ian hadn't wanted to press her on the matter. He was already feeling mildly guilty about pressuring her into taking the job in the first place.

Not *too* guilty, though. This arrangement was exactly what Annie and Abby needed. Ian had a great feeling about it, all around. If he'd been a little overenthusiastic, it was only because he'd been desperate. At the end of his parental rope. That was going to change, though. Starting today…right now, in fact.

"Actually." Rachel's gaze flitted from the bicycle to the boxes and back again. She tightened her grip on the worn leather suitcase. "This is it."

"Oh." She seemed so visibly uncomfortable with the conversation that Ian made every effort to hide his surprise, not wanting to make her feel worse. "I see. Well, great. I'll just help you get all of this to the carriage house and you'll be all set."

"Thank you." Rachel smiled but seemed to avoid his gaze as she made her way toward the footpath that led around the side of the main house.

Not that Ian—Mr. *I'll triple your salary!*—could blame her. What he'd intended as generosity, edged with perhaps a bit of mania, had probably come across as him throwing his weight around, intimidating her with his wealth and privilege. He supposed he'd made a jerk out of himself, again, by hurling money at her like that. He needed to work on trying to be a better person. A person with patience, grace and a sunny outlook.

A person more like Rachel.

Although, as he attempted to juggle the boxes and walk her bike down the footpath at the same time, he realized that he didn't actually know Rachel very well. Not really.

Her wariness about the door being unlocked had caught him off guard. This was Spring Forest, after all. Aside from the unfortunate incident last year when Birdie and Bunny Whitaker from Furever Paws Animal Rescue had found out that their brother Gator, who they had trusted to handle their investment portfolio, was actually embezzling their money, their little town was pretty much crime-free. Especially the neighborhood of Kingdom Creek. Locked doors just weren't a thing here.

But was that him, not considering what life was

like for other people again? He couldn't claim he knew what it was like to be a single woman living alone. And a beautiful one, at that. Locked doors might be a perfectly normal way of life for her—a simple, standard precaution that was par for the course, especially since she was new to the area and might not realize how safe she was here. But no matter how hard he tried to understand her perspective, he couldn't manage to wrap his head around the fact that she had so little baggage.

Was that a bad sign? Did she travel light specifically so she could pack and leave at a moment's notice? Maybe that was how she'd ended up in North Carolina to begin with. She'd never actually explained why she'd left Virginia.

Stop it. He was being ridiculous. Marianne had given Rachel an impeccable reference. She never would have gotten a job at Spring Forest Day School without passing a thorough background check. Ian had seen for himself what a difference she could make in his daughters' lives. If he was judging her for not having much by way of material possessions, it just meant that he'd spent a few too many years in Ivy League schools, gated communities and country clubs. It was a little sobering to realize how his perceptions of people had shifted, without him even realizing it. He'd become one of

the elite who he'd always thought were so out of
touch with reality.

That's not what he wanted for his girls. Not really. Serena was the one who'd been born with a
silver spoon in her mouth, not him. She'd wanted
Abby and Annie to grow up the same way that she
had—music lessons, all the best schools, summer
camp with ponies and swim parties at the members-
only neighborhood pool. When she had pitched him
on that lifestyle for their growing family, Ian had
hardly needed convincing. That sort of childhood
sounded idyllic.

But all the wealth and material possessions in
the world hadn't been able to protect his daughters
from the heartbreak of losing their mother. Privilege
didn't protect them—and he didn't want them to
grow up believing that money solved every problem.
Not when he knew now with utter certainty that it
didn't. Sometimes, it just created more issues, more
complications, more expectations.

There wasn't anything wrong with living a simple life. In fact, *simple* sounded pretty fantastic right
about now.

Ian parked the bicycle beneath the shade of the
cozy porch of the carriage house and carried the
boxes inside. Rachel had already tucked her suitcase
in the bedroom and was moving through the house,

tying back the eyelet curtains Serena had ordered from a fancy boutique in Brevard.

"Everything okay?" he asked.

"Great. It's lovely. I can't believe you offered to let me stay here." She bit her lip, gaze flicking toward the bedroom like a nervous little butterfly.

Ian set the boxes down on the smooth pine coffee table. "But?"

She winced, an unspoken apology. "But the window in the kitchen doesn't close all the way. I think it's stuck."

He scrubbed a hand over his face. *Dang it.* She was right, of course. He'd known about that issue and he'd meant to take care of it, but then he'd completely forgotten. Like everything else these days that didn't have to do with work or the girls, it had slipped right through the cracks. "You're completely right. Would you believe a month ago I caught a raccoon trying to get in here through that window?"

Rachel's eyes went wide. "A raccoon?"

"A *pregnant* raccoon." She'd waddled from the wooded area out back, straight toward the carriage house, looking for a cozy place to have her babies. For a brief, insane moment, Ian had almost let her. He'd sympathized with her plight as a single parent, poor thing.

"I'm not going to wake up with a myriad of woodland creatures beside me in bed tonight, am

I?" Rachel laughed, but her smile didn't quite reach her eyes.

First the lock on the door, now the window.

She's afraid. The realization crashed over Ian like a wave on one of the sugar-sand beaches of the Outer Banks. Rachel was frightened.

Of some*thing*?

Some*one*?

Neither option was palatable to Ian. He felt his hands clench, completely of their own volition. The urge to protect her from whatever invisible force threatened to encroach on this little slice of Spring Forest heaven clawed at his insides.

He told himself it didn't mean anything. He felt the same protectiveness toward Annie and Abby, after all. He couldn't—*wouldn't*—stand to see them hurt in any way. Wasn't that precisely how Rachel had come into their lives to begin with? There were some things even the most protective father couldn't keep at bay. But that wouldn't stop him from trying.

Still, the way his teeth suddenly clenched until they ached took him by surprise. No one was in any sort of danger. There was no threat. Kingdom Creek was one of the safest places on earth.

It wasn't until later, after Ian had gone to the hardware store for supplies and come back to fix the window with his own two hands while Rachel

organized her books—a curious mixture of litera-
ture, children's classics like *The Velveteen Rabbit*
and hardback texts on childhood development—
that he understood why the urge to protect her had
caught him so off guard.

He'd forgotten what it felt like to be so aware of
the blood pumping through his veins. The clenching of his jaw. The feeling of need...

Ian had been numb for so long that he'd grown
accustomed to it. In the few days that he'd known
Rachel, a thaw had begun. Something inside of him
was shifting, breaking apart and coming ever-so-
slowly back to life.

He felt his teeth grind together as he set aside his
screwdriver and pushed hard on the window's nar-
row wooden frame—one, two, three times, until it
finally slammed shut tight.

Rachel jumped. Her hand flew to her throat, but
then she took in the sight of the closed window. Her
features relaxed, and Ian felt another twinge deep
inside. He swallowed it down and counted slowly to
ten until the familiar iciness returned to his chest,
his gut, his heart.

He didn't want to start feeling things again, least
of all for his new nanny. This wasn't about him.
It was about Abby and Annie—his sweet, sweet
Annie, who needed to find her voice again. And
Abby, who'd somehow come to believe it was her

responsibility to shield her twin sister from the outside world.

But then he remembered what Rachel had told him a few nights ago.

The best possible thing a parent can do to help a child overcome shyness is to show them how it's done... When she sees you being open and friendly around others, Annie will feel more comfortable doing the same.

Maybe he didn't have much of a choice. If he shut down every time he felt the slightest twinge of connection, how would Annie ever learn to open her heart again?

"All fixed." Ian waved the screwdriver toward the window. "Nothing's going to sneak in here and surprise you."

"Thank you so much." Rachel slid the last of the books on the shelf and dusted off her hands. Relief was written all over her lovely face.

Although, should he be thinking about Rachel in those terms? Probably not.

Ian's chest stirred again, and he realized what he'd begun to feel was more than simple connection. More than just a protective streak. As much as he hated to admit it, even to himself, the long-forgotten sensation that seemed to come over him every time Rachel was near was longing. He knew that ache. It had just been a long, long time since it had wrapped itself around his battered heart.

Rachel tucked a stray curl of shimmering auburn hair behind her ear, seemingly oblivious to the effect she had on him. Why, oh why, did it have to be her? "I'll sleep better tonight for sure."

Ian forced a smile. *That makes one of us.*

Chapter Five

Rachel spent the rest of the weekend adjusting to her new reality. She was no longer a teaching assistant at a day care center, and she didn't go home to a shabby, sad hotel room at the end of every day. She had her own little house now. It didn't technically belong to her, obviously, but it was hers and hers alone—at least for now. And she loved every single thing about it.

She loved how it was set back from the road, hidden from view of the street. Between the trees surrounding the property—slender loblolly pines, leafy sweet gums and magnolias, heady with fragrance—

and Ian's towering Tudor-style manor, it was impossible to know the carriage house existed. It was like the sweetest of secrets, the safe space she'd been craving for a long, long time.

As private as it was, Rachel's life became immediately intertwined with all three of the residents in the main house. In the mornings, just as the sun was peeking over the Smoky Mountains in the distance, layering the sky in whisper-soft shades of blue, she twisted her hair into a messy bun and made the short trek from her front door to the kitchen entrance of Ian's sprawling home. She fumbled with the coffee maker as Ian headed out for his morning run, the girls still snug in their beds. Despite every effort not to, Rachel often found herself watching him jog down the footpath toward the road with an easy rhythm to his movements—muscles moving and shifting beneath his fitted T-shirt as she sipped rich French roast.

It was only in those quiet predawn moments that Rachel sometimes wondered if she'd made a terrible mistake. There was just something so unnerving about witnessing Ian's private morning routine. So *intimate*. Without Annie and Abby swirling around his long, lean legs, as they did when he came home from work, Rachel felt overly aware that he wasn't just a father. Or just a boss. He was a man.

A man who could run three miles in the time

it took her to drink two cups of coffee and get the table set for the twins' breakfast. A man who returned from those morning sprints smelling like pine and morning dew, his body loose and relaxed as he headed upstairs to shower and dress for the day's work. A man who once almost left the house with his tie slightly askew...

Until Rachel volunteered to retie it for him. There'd been a moment when she'd caught him watching her intently as her fingertips moved deftly over the smooth silk of his necktie—Hermès, according to the dark blue label on its underside. Rachel had been spot-on about that. Her gaze flicked toward his and she'd suddenly been unable to breathe. Unable to move, even though she could usually tie a necktie half asleep and with her eyes closed given that she'd helped her father with his tie more times than she could count back when she'd been a teenager.

Two breathless seconds passed. Maybe three. And then muscle memory had kicked in. Her hands seemed to move of their own accord, finishing the job while her eyes stayed locked with Ian's. When the knot was finished, she rested her palm against his tie, flattening it in place, and she could feel his heartbeat pounding against her fingertips as his eyes slowly drifted shut. A magic spell seemed to wrap itself around them, right there in the kitchen. As lush and intoxicating as one of the great magnolias, swaying in the cool Carolina breeze.

Then Abby had burst into the room with quiet little Annie tiptoeing behind her, breaking the strange spell with their tousled blond heads, their baby powder scent and their matching girly pajamas—pink with tiny white polka dots and ruffled trim. Rachel had never been so happy to see two small children in her life.

That had been two days ago. Since then, Ian hadn't asked for help with his tie, and Rachel hadn't dared to offer. It remained an isolated incident, but the memory of it lingered in every quiet moment. So much so that Rachel found herself babbling every time she was alone with him, just to fill the loaded silences.

No babbling was necessary on Friday afternoon, though, as Rachel sat at the breakfast table in the kitchen of the main house, wielding a crayon alongside the twins. Earlier in the day, Rachel had taken Abby and Annie on an outing to Chapter One, the charming new bookstore in downtown Spring Forest.

Since the girls were now spending so much time at home instead of being in preschool for most of the day, she wanted to make sure they got out and about to work on proper socialization. Rachel had promised to buy them each one book and then set them loose in the cozy children's area in the back of the store to pick something out. Abby had bounced from shelf to shelf, while Annie stayed close to Rachel, clinging to her skirt with a tiny toddler hand. In the end, Rachel had helped them select pseudomatching coloring books—a kitten-themed one for Abby and a book filled with puppies to color for Annie.

"Both of you are doing such a great job," she said as she plucked a purple crayon from the jumbo-sized green-and-yellow box in the center of the table. Each twin had torn a page out of her respective coloring book for Rachel. She was currently alternating her attention back and forth between a fluffy kitten playing with a ball of yarn and a dalmatian in a bubble bath. "I like your puppy's pink collar, Annie. How did you choose that color?"

Annie glanced up from her artwork. Rachel smiled and waited…

She'd learned a long time ago that getting a shy child to engage was mostly just a waiting game. It took patience to draw a quiet toddler out of her shell. After a few seconds of silence, most adults simply gave up and moved on. Rachel had what she called the six-second rule when working with shy children. She liked to ask the child a question, give them an animated, engaged look and then wait at least six seconds for a response…sometimes longer.

It worked nearly every time.

The point was to build up the child's confidence, making sure the child knew that Rachel was genuinely interested in what they had to say so they eventually felt more comfortable with a back-and-forth conversation. Cutting them off before they felt safe responding did far more harm than good.

Annie blinked up at Rachel with wide blue eyes—eyes glittering with little gold flecks that reminded Rachel so much of Ian that her heart gave a not-so-little squeeze—and said nothing.

Four seconds passed.

Then five.

Annie shifted her attention back toward her coloring book, and Rachel held her breath as she counted to six in her head.

"Me like pink," Annie said.

Her voice was scarcely louder than the scratch of her crayon moving back and forth across the thin paper of her coloring book, but it filled Rachel's chest with warmth all the same.

"I like pink too," she said.

"Me too!" Abby bopped up and down in her chair as she tossed a yellow crayon aside and reached for a pink one.

Just as she started coloring the kitten on her page pink, Rachel held up a finger. "Oopsie! Just one crayon out of the box at a time, remember?"

"Oopsie," the little girl echoed. "I 'member."

She crammed the yellow crayon back in the box just as Ian walked through the back door.

"Hey, there. How are my girls?" He tossed his car keys on the kitchen counter and tugged his tie loose, just enough to unfasten the top button of his dress shirt, as he strode toward the table.

How are my girls?

It was his standard greeting when he got home from work, and even though Rachel knew it was directed at Abby and Annie, happiness zinged through her every time she heard it. Which was ridiculous. She wasn't Ian Parsons's "girl," and she never would be.

Nor do I want to be, she reminded herself.

"What's this?" Ian said, glancing down at the twins' colorful pictures.

The styles of drawing were as different as the girls themselves. Abby's kitten was a colorful blob, barely still recognizable as feline. Annie, on the other hand, had carefully colored within the lines—as best a chubby toddler fist could manage.

"We went to Chapter One today and bought coloring books," Rachel said.

"Kitties!" Abby held up her book for her daddy to see and promptly began meowing at the top of her lungs.

Annie remained as silently stoic as a Saint Bernard.

"A pink kitten. Very nice." Ian ruffled Abby's hair.

She resumed coloring with her pink crayon, filling the entire page with broad strokes, meowing again every few seconds.

"And what did you pick to color, Annie?" Ian asked, squatting so they were eye to eye.

Annie's gaze flicked toward him, but she didn't answer.

Ian glanced at Rachel and she gave him an encouraging nod. *Be patient. The six-second rule, remember?*

She'd already explained the importance of waiting to Ian. Even though she could tell it pained him to just sit quietly and wait for a response, he seemed to be giving it his best try. When Annie quietly picked up her crayon and began filling in the bow atop the puppy's head without saying anything, a muscle in Ian's jaw ticked.

Rachel nodded again, prompting him to give Annie another cue.

"I'm listening, sweetheart," he said.

Annie woofed in a tiny, bell-like voice, and Ian's face split into a wide grin.

It was the tiniest of triumphs. A bark wasn't even a real word, but baby steps were still progress. Annie had responded verbally to him, and the heartfelt gratitude that Rachel saw in Ian's amber eyes when he mouthed *thank you* to her over the top of Annie's head made her heart swell.

"You know what? We should do something fun tonight." Ian straightened. "It's Friday. How about a family trip to Pins and Pints?"

Abby thrust her pink crayon in the air and let out an immediate meow that somehow sounded like a yes, while Annie smiled up at her father. Ian lit up in response to their joy, as relaxed and happy as Rachel had ever seen him.

"What's Pins and Pints?" she asked as she started helping the girls straighten up the art supplies. She probably needed to help them get changed and freshened up before they left for family night with their dad.

"It's an old-fashioned bowling alley." Ian lowered his voice and curved a hand around his mouth so the twins couldn't see what he was saying, which probably wasn't necessary since their little brows were furrowed in concentration while they organized their crayons. "In the evenings, it's also a bar, but if we get there early enough, we'll be in and out while it's still family friendly."

Rachel winked. "I hear you. I'll help the girls get ready and you can be on your way."

Ian's smile dimmed a bit. "You don't want to come with us?"

"Um…"

He held up a hand. "Sorry. I apologize. It's Friday night. You probably have plans. I didn't mean to make you feel obligated."

Rachel didn't have a single plan for the evening, unless a book, a bubble bath and going to bed early counted. "You didn't. It's just that you called it a family trip to Pins and Pints, and well…"

She wasn't family. Rachel hadn't been part of a real family for a long, long time.

A line etched between Ian's eyebrows. "I meant you, too, of course."

Rachel's heart did a pathetic loop-de-loop. She was sure he didn't mean anything by it. She was the *nanny*.

But still, it was nice being thought of as anything close to a member of the family. Even if she knew she couldn't stay in the pretty little carriage house long.

It's best not to stay anywhere *long. Remember the plan.*

"I probably shouldn't," she said as a familiar weight settled on her chest.

"Oh." Ian nodded. "Okay. I understand."

He really didn't. He couldn't possibly, but Rachel couldn't spell it out, even if she'd wanted to.

She gathered the coloring books in her arms so she wouldn't have to see the confused expression on his face, but then a tiny voice stopped her in her tracks.

"Please." Annie peered up at Rachel with pleading eyes. A rare moment of self-expression. Actual verbalization!

How could she possibly say no to that?

"What do you say?" Ian said, arching a brow at her as he rested his hand atop Annie's blond head.

It's the right thing to do—for Annie's sake. It doesn't mean you're getting attached. But as Rachel looked into Ian's eyes, that swoony, fluttery feeling came over her again, just like when she'd helped him with his tie.

She'd lived here a matter of days and she was already in trouble, wasn't she?

The weight on her chest suddenly felt as heavy as the bowling ball she'd no doubt be wielding soon. "Sure, I'd love to come."

Pins and Pints had been around since Ian was just a kid. Until Calum Ramsey took it over three years ago and overhauled the ten-lane bowling alley, it had been so perfectly preserved in its original, vintage state that Ian had always felt like he'd been stepping back in time when he'd pushed through the doors.

He'd had his first kiss in lane four—an innocent peck on Mary Jane Wheeler's cheek after she'd beaten the pants off him three times in a row. Ian had been fifteen years old, and now here he was, seventeen years later, feeling even more like a nervous kid in the presence of Rachel Gray than he had with a sophomore cheerleader with braces on her teeth and a freakishly good curveball.

"Wow, this place is really something." Rachel's gaze swept from the bowling lanes to the right of the entrance, past the shoe rental station toward the mahogany bar that swept clear to the other end of the building.

Since they'd arrived early—more than two hours before the food trucks and live band normally set up out front—less than half the seats at the bar were occupied. Bowling balls dropping and rolling along the smooth wooden floor, followed by the clatter of pins and happy laughter, were typically the only sounds that made up the soundtrack of Pins and Pints during family hour.

"The girls love it," Ian said, shoving his hands in the pockets of his jeans as Abby skipped toward the counter where the bowling alley's owner, Calum Ramsey, and his fiancée, Lucy Tucker, were looking far too deliriously happy about passing out two-toned borrowed shoes.

Of course, Ian knew that it wasn't the shoes that were putting those dreamy smiles on their faces. He was just having a hard time remembering what it felt like to be so in love...so full of hopes and dreams for the future.

Had he and Serena *ever* looked at each other the

way Calum was gazing at Lucy as he placed a hand reverently over the swell of her pregnant belly?

Ian wasn't so sure.

A stab of guilt pricked his conscience as he and Rachel caught up to the twins at the shoe counter. Serena was dead. He shouldn't be thinking about her or their relationship in anything but glowing terms.

"Hey there, Ian." Calum removed his hand from Lucy's belly and held it up in a wave.

Lucy glowed in that way that all blissful brides and expectant moms seemed to. Ian's throat grew tight for reasons he didn't want to think too much about.

"Hello, Calum. Lucy." Ian nodded at them both and then turned toward Rachel. His hand somehow seemed to move of its own accord and find its way to the small of her back. "Have you two had a chance to meet Rachel Gray yet?"

"No, I don't believe we have," Lucy said, eyes dancing. "But didn't I see you shopping with the twins at Chapter One earlier today?"

"Yes. I'm the girls' nanny," Rachel said, tongue practically tripping over the words in her haste to get them out.

"Oh. Of course." Lucy nodded, and the hint of surprise that flickered in her gaze was just enough to make Ian realize that she and Calum had proba-bly assumed that he and Rachel were a couple who had come out on a date. A couple deeply involved enough for her to go on outings with his daughters.

He removed his hand from the small of Rachel's back and raked it through his hair before shoving it in his pocket.

"It's so nice to meet you, Rachel. I own the bookstore," Lucy said.

"And I run things around here," Calum said.

"Normally, I would've popped out of my office to greet you, but I was stuck on the phone with my book distributor while you were in." Lucy flashed another beaming smile. "You must be new to Spring Forest," Lucy said.

"I am." Rachel nodded. "Your store is great—I can't wait to go back and explore it another time. I suppose I haven't had much of a chance to really get out and see the town since I've gotten here."

Calum shot Ian a mock glare. "Working her that hard, are you, Parsons?"

"Oh, no. It's not that. It's just…" Rachel let out a nervous laugh. "I'm something of a homebody."

Ian felt himself frown as her face flooded with color. Had she left the carriage house at all during her time off in the past few days?

He didn't think so. Then again, what Rachel did on her off hours was none of his business. She showed up on time every morning and did a superlative job—not to mention, Annie and Abby adored her. That was what really mattered.

Case in point: Annie was currently sidling up next to her nanny, wrapping her slender arms around one of Rachel's legs, bunching her floral skirt in the process. Rachel didn't seem to mind a bit.

"Look, Daddy!" Abby tugged on Ian's shirt sleeve, dragging his attention away from his winsome yet slightly mysterious nanny. He followed the aim of his daughter's little pointer finger until he found himself looking at a familiar feline face.

"Olly-ver," she said, enunciating with care as she pointed at the missing cat poster pinned to the wall behind Calum's head.

Calum and Lucy turned in unison to look at the picture of the kitty's orange face with its pink triangle nose and jade-colored eyes. *Find me, already*, they seemed to say. Or possibly, Ian was projecting. Abby had pointed out the missing posters to him so many times now that he was beginning to see cats in his sleep.

"I'm guessing Brooklyn Hobbs still hasn't found her cat," Ian said.

Calum shook his head. "Not that I've heard."

Lucy nodded. "And we've had our eyes peeled for the poor thing."

"We have too," Rachel said.

"Especially a certain someone." Ian's gaze cut toward Abby.

"Meow," she promptly said in a singsong voice.

All of a sudden, a loud woof erupted from behind the counter. Both Abby's and Annie's eyes went as big as saucers.

"That's just Buttercup. I guess you tricked her into thinking you were a cat, Abby." Lucy laughed as a young golden retriever rose up on her hind legs and placed her front paws on the counter.

Annie let out a giggle the likes of which Ian hadn't heard come out of her mouth in months. Warmth filled his chest as Rachel scooped Annie into her arms so she could get a better look at the dog.

"Buttercup silly," Annie whispered, dimples flashing in her chubby little cheeks.

"She can definitely be silly at times." Lucy winked. "How about I let her out so you all can get a better look at her?"

Lucy opened the bottom half of the Dutch door at the end of the counter, and Buttercup bounded out of the shoe rental station, fluffy gold tail swinging back and forth. Rachel lowered Annie to the ground, and the second her feet hit the floor, Buttercup ran over and licked one of her hands with a swipe of her big pink tongue. Annie giggled, and the sound of her laughter seemed to squeeze Ian's heart like a vise.

"What a sweet dog," Rachel said as Buttercup positioned her head directly under her hand so Rachel had no choice but to pet her.

"She's my baby." Lucy rested a hand over her heart and then cast a meaningful glance at her baby bump. "For now, anyway."

"Who are you kidding? That dog will always be your baby." Calum wrapped an arm around Lucy's waist and pulled her close. "And I wouldn't have it any other way. Buttercup and our little one will be best friends."

Lucy beamed, and again, Ian found himself feeling oddly hollow inside. He swallowed the feeling down and pasted on a smile. "How are the wedding plans coming along?"

"Great. The day can't get here soon enough as far as I'm concerned." Calum pressed a kiss to the top of Lucy's head.

"Buttercup is going to be our flower girl," Lucy said.

Abby's dimples flashed—a little different from her sister's but just as sweet. "But she's a dog."

Lucy shrugged. "She can still be a flower girl, don't you think?"

Abby laughed so loud that Buttercup's ears pricked into two high triangles on either side of her golden head.

"I think that sounds lovely." Rachel's eyes sparkled. "You'll make a wonderful flower girl, won't you, Buttercup?"

Buttercup's tail wagged even harder, beating against Abby's and Annie's legs as they laughed. The dog panted and her mouth seemed to curve into a smile, and then she trotted off a short distance for a better view of the lanes. Abby grabbed Annie's hand and they skipped after the goofy dog.

"Your girls really love animals. Have you ever thought about adopting a pet?" Lucy said, rubbing her belly in slow, gentle circles.

Ian felt his eyebrows raise almost all the way to his hairline. "A dog?" Was she serious? He was barely keeping things together as it was. There was no possible way he could add an animal to the mix. It wasn't as if the girls were old enough to really be able to help with feeding and walks. "I don't think so."

Ever the advocate for fostering or adopting homeless pets, Lucy pressed on. "It doesn't have to be a dog. Abby seems pretty partial to cats."

"Correct, but Annie prefers dogs." Rachel slid Ian a meaningful glance.

He glanced from her to Lucy and back again. "How is it that you two just met and I already feel like I'm being tag-teamed?"

Lucy shot Rachel a wink, and Rachel laughed.

"We are *not* adopting a pet, much less two," Ian

said. It was strange how his tongue didn't even trip over the word *we*, as if they were truly in this together. Like a family…like a *couple*. Warmth percolated between them—an ease that made him feel loose and languid. Happy, even. He had to stop himself from placing his hand on the small of Rachel's back again.

Inappropriate, much? She's the nanny, not your life partner.

She'd made such a difference in the lives of his girls in just a matter of days. He was confusing gratitude with attraction. That's all.

"I'm outnumbered enough as it is," he said, jamming his hands into the back pockets of his jeans.

Calum's gaze was a little too knowing for Ian's liking, so he was grateful when Rachel interrupted the loaded silence by rattling off her shoe size along with those of the girls. Fifteen minutes later, the four of them were settled at the lane farthest to the right. Annie and Abby stood side by side, facing the pins, while Buttercup wagged her approval from the sidelines.

Annie squatted and pushed her ball forward. It rolled in a slow crawl toward the end of the lane, finally sending half the pins clattering to the floor. Instead of Annie trying to pick up the spare herself, Abby tossed her hot-pink ball onto the ground. It landed with a thud before curving into a mirror image of the path that Annie's ball had taken and wiping out the remaining pins.

The twins threw their arms over their heads and jumped up and down. Buttercup's tail *thump-thumped* against the floor, and her mouth curved into a wide doggy smile, pink tongue lolling.

Rachel glanced from the girls to the dog and then back at Ian.

"Don't say it," he said, biting back a grin. "It all paints a really cute picture, I know. But Lucy has spent months training that dog. They don't come home straight from the shelter ready to work at a bowling alley and acting like the canine equivalent of Mary Poppins."

Rachel held up her hands. "I didn't say a word."

"Although, a few of the moms at my Parents of Twins group mentioned that the local shelter allows kids to come visit the dogs and cats." Ian could handle *visiting*. Maybe the girls could take one of the dogs on a walk or play with some kittens. Annie and Abby would certainly enjoy it.

Rachel bit back a smile. "Again, I'm not saying a word."

Out of the corner of his eye, Ian noticed his daughters stopping to visit Buttercup on their way to the ball return. Annie hugged the big golden retriever around the neck and pressed a kiss to her furry head.

"It's only a visit," he said.

"Absolutely." Rachel nodded, but the way her eyes danced told Ian if he wasn't careful, he was going to end up with at least one more living, breathing soul depending on him for everything. The fact that she wasn't overtly encouraging him to adopt a pet somehow made her amused expression even more persuasive.

Ian looked away before he started filling out pet adoption paperwork in his head. Unfortunately, he accidentally locked eyes with Buttercup, who could have been a poster dog for adorable, adoptable homeless animals. *Love me*, her melting puppy-dog eyes seemed to say.

He glared at the dog and cut his gaze toward the lane, where the twins were now tag-teaming the turn that was supposed to be Abby's.

Ian felt his shoulders go tense. "Is it bad that I let them help each other? Am I doing more unintended harm to Annie's confidence?"

Rachel turned toward him, smile fading. "Ian, you're not harming your children. I hope nothing I've said has given you that impression. You're doing your best and learning new techniques to help your girls thrive. In my book, that makes you a wonderful father."

Relief coursed through him along with a warm feeling he'd begun to associate specifically with

Rachel. It reminded him of tipping his face toward a sunrise and seeing the sky washed in soft tones of pink on an early morning run. "You really think so?"

"Of course I do." She reached for his hand and squeezed it tight.

Electricity skittered over every inch of his skin. Just as he was wondering if she felt it, too, Rachel let out a breathy gasp and her eyes went liquid for a beat. Ian's fingertips seemed to move of their own accord, weaving themselves through hers. At the base of Rachel's willowy neck, he could see the quiver of her pulse, as quick and delicate as the wings of a butterfly. From the way it was jumping, she seemed just as caught up in this moment as he was.

Somewhere nearby, a bowling ball banged on the floor. Rachel's hand disentangled itself from his and flew to her heart.

"That startled me," she said, and Ian wasn't sure if she meant the sudden noise or the fact that he'd just held her hand—and she'd let him. Whatever brief intimacy had blossomed between them seemed to slip through his fingers.

He shoved his hands back inside his pockets. "Me too."

He gave her his best attempt at a smile, but she'd already wrapped her arms around herself and turned back toward the children.

It was for the best, really. He couldn't screw this up for the girls. Their needs were far more important than his. Ian couldn't, *wouldn't*, ruin things for them by becoming the world's worst cliché—the dad who fell for the nanny.

Chapter Six

Rachel did her best to keep to herself over the weekend so she could give Ian some proper family time with his children. Not that their bowling outing hadn't been the perfect, cozy night out for two adults and a pair of precious twin toddlers, because it had. Very much so, actually.

Hence Rachel's hesitance to show her face for the remainder of the weekend.

It was bad enough that she was getting more attached to Abby and Annie with each passing day. She couldn't do the same with Ian. Staying in Spring Forest permanently had never been part of her plan. This was just a stopover, a place to try and regain her equilibrium after a wobbly few years. She was supposed to be taking a much needed breath, saving her money and coming up with a real agenda for her future.

What she was *not* supposed to be doing was holding hands with her boss and thinking about how being with him and his daughters made her feel at last like she belonged somewhere. *Really* belonged.

So Rachel pretended not to hear the tiny knocks on her door Sunday afternoon when Ian, Annie and Abby were having a tea party on a blanket in the backyard. She buried her face in her book and didn't dare peek beyond the eyelet curtains in her bedroom. When she stepped outside Monday morning and found a plastic teacup and saucer sitting on her doorstep, her heart gave a forbidden little tug. Inside the flowery cup was a handful of chocolate kisses wrapped in silvery foil.

Those little girls were going to break her heart if she wasn't careful. Clearly, this was a situation that required chocolate. Immediately. She removed the wrapper from one of the kisses, popped the candy into her mouth and strode to the back door of the main house, bracing herself to face Ian for the first time since their sweet, intimate moment at the bowling alley.

"Good morning," she said as breezily as she could

manage as she pushed through the door and spotted a figure standing by the coffee maker.

And then she blinked, because it wasn't Ian. No broad, muscular shoulders. No charming morning stubble. No tiny, clingy running shorts that she was always dangerously tempted to stare at, agog.

Instead, Elma turned to face her, sipping from Ian's favorite coffee cup—the one with the photo of Abby and Annie in matching pumpkin costumes from last Halloween.

The chocolate kiss seemed to lodge in Rachel's throat. She gulped it down and managed a weak attempt at a smile. "Good morning, Elma."

Elma went completely and utterly still as her gaze traveled from Rachel's messy bun, which probably screamed "just rolled out of bed," all the way down to her tank top, her softest pair of jeans and her pink ballerina flats that had begun to form a hole in the right toe. She may as well have been wearing pajamas, bunny slippers and a sign around her neck that said I SLEPT HERE LAST NIGHT.

"Good morning," Elma said coolly. The only outward sign of any emotion she might be experiencing upon seeing Rachel walk into her son-in-law's kitchen at six in the morning was a tiny slosh of coffee that spilled over the rim of her trembling coffee mug. "What was your name again? Rebecca?"

"It's Rachel." She smiled as she clutched the teacup to her chest as if it were a security blanket made of chipped plastic. "It's lovely to see you again. I'm guessing you might be wondering why I'm here."

Elma's raised eyebrow said it all.

"I work here now. I'm Abby and Annie's nanny." She held the teacup up as evidence.

"Their *nanny*?" Elma sniffed. "Well, isn't that interesting? I tried to tell Ian that the children would be better off staying at home with me while he went to work, but he insisted they needed to be in preschool so they could make friends. It seems he's changed his mind."

"The girls are just taking a break. Ian fully intends to enroll them in school again…soon. Annie and Abby just need a little time to adjust to their family situation." Rachel swallowed hard. She definitely didn't want to be the one who had to explain to Elma that her grandchildren were struggling with the loss of their mom. "I know Ian meant to talk to you about everything as soon as you returned from your trip. I'm guessing you haven't had a chance to discuss things yet."

"I just got home last night. I got up early to make cinnamon rolls to surprise everyone this morning." She let out a world-weary sigh, as if she'd just returned from circumnavigating the globe instead of shopping for antiques in Asheville. "Now I'm the one that's surprised. Can I ask why you're sneaking in through the back door instead of arriving at work via the front entrance?"

"Oh. Well…" Rachel shifted her weight from one foot to the other. She'd sort of thought the fact that she was living on the premises had been implied, but apparently not. Well, if she needed to spell it out… "I'm staying in the carriage house. Since Ian occasionally works long hours, he suggested it might be easier if I was just a stone's throw away."

Elma said nothing. Rachel had thought she might be glad to hear that Rachel wasn't actually staying in the main house, but she didn't seem relieved in the slightest. In fact, the color appeared to be slowly draining from her face, as if the news of Rachel moving into the carriage house was even worse than if she'd just climbed out of Ian's bed.

"I usually pop over early in the mornings so Ian can go on a run without worrying about leaving the girls by themselves." She was just babbling now. Why did she feel guilty even though she'd done nothing wrong?

Rachel reached into the teacup for another candy but came up empty. There wasn't enough chocolate in the world to get her through this uncomfortable conversation anyway.

"The carriage house was meant for my retirement," Elma said quietly. "That's what Serena told me, but I suppose things have changed. Nothing is the same anymore."

The older woman's shoulders sagged, and Rachel crumbled a little bit inside. Elma was hurting... *clearly.* No wonder Ian had been dragging his feet about setting firmer boundaries and had put off talking to Elma about her job as the girls' nanny.

Rachel set the teacup down on the kitchen counter and glanced at the fresh pan of cinnamon rolls situated on a neatly folded gingham-checked dish towel. The icing on them was at least an inch thick. If she hadn't been so concerned for Elma, the comforting scents of cinnamon and warm dough might have made her moan out loud.

"Those look delicious. You're a wonderful cook, Elma. Ian and the girls are very lucky to have you," Rachel said, sliding her gaze toward Elma.

The compliment seemed to catch the older woman off guard. Her lips flashed a smile that vanished almost as quickly as it appeared. "Thank you, although I doubt Ian agrees with you. Most of the time, I think he considers me more of a burden than a help."

"I'm sure that's not true."

"No, it was my daughter who wanted me around, not Ian. And now she's gone—and everyone is moving on. Everyone except me."

Rachel shifted her weight from one ballerina flat

to the other. She probably shouldn't be inserting herself into Ian's personal family business.

Scratch that—she *definitely* shouldn't. But Elma had lost a daughter. Rachel knew what it was like to lose a loved one. It was messy and complicated, but most of all, it was lonely—such a lonely, lonely experience that Rachel would never wish it on anyone.

Rachel had been just a tiny baby when her mom passed away, but Emily Gray's absence had left a mark on her every bit as raw and real as if she'd actually remembered what it had felt like to be cradled in her mother's arms. Or had known the sound of her mother's laughter…the taste of her favorite chocolate cake recipe. Sometimes, Rachel even wondered if she still would have ended up so thoroughly ruining her own life if her mother had never been buried all those years ago.

But she knew better than to go down that road. What's done was done. The past was the past… It just didn't always feel that way when she was still actively running away from it.

"No one will ever replace your daughter." Rachel reached to give Elma's hand a squeeze. "That's not why I took this job. You have my word. I'm here for the girls—as their nanny and nothing more— because they need my help. But I don't have a permanent place in their lives. *You* do."

Elma looked out at the carriage house through

the window above the sink, nodding slowly. Then she reached into the cabinet for a plate, carefully placed one of the warm cinnamon rolls on it and handed it to Rachel.

"I'll admit you have a calming effect on Abby, and Annie does seem to come out of her shell a bit when you're around," Elma said with no small amount of reluctance.

"Thank you." Rachel took a bite of the cinnamon roll. It was doughy and sweet and tasted so much like home that it made her throat go thick.

This is not *your home, and it never will be.*

"Again, you don't have to worry. The carriage house will still be here for your retirement. I'm only here for a little while, and there's nothing between Ian and me." She swallowed around the lump in her throat. "You have my word."

Ian stood in the hallway just around the corner from the kitchen, willing himself not to clear his throat. Or step on the one plank of the hardwood floor that always seemed to creak. Or do anything else to give away his presence to Elma and Rachel.

He had no business whatsoever listening in on their conversation, obviously. Ian was keenly aware that his behavior was problematic, but he couldn't seem to stop himself. The vulnerability in Rachel's tone as she spoke to his mother-in-law had held him spellbound. She always kept herself so tightly guarded, and he hadn't been able to resist listening to her actually open up. He'd only meant to catch a word or two. He wanted to know her…really know her. But it had been years since Ian had been interested in a woman. He didn't know how to go about it anymore. Sometimes when he was around Rachel, it was all he could do to form complete sentences, much less develop any sort of meaningful connection.

Plus, she was the children's *nanny*. He shouldn't even be thinking in terms of getting to know her better.

And yet…

As soon as she'd uttered those fateful words, Ian's heart seemed to freeze.

I'm only here for a little while, and there's nothing between Ian and me. You have my word.

The moment he'd heard them, Ian had gone hollow inside. His ribs grew tight, and he felt like he couldn't breathe. He had a sharp twinge in his chest. It almost felt like an acute case of homesickness.

Which made no sense whatsoever. Ian already had a home. He was standing right inside of it. And he knew perfectly well that the goal was to get the twins back in school. The nanny arrangement was never meant to be permanent.

"Good morning, everyone," he said, doing his

best to paste a smile on his face as he propelled himself into the kitchen.

Enough with the lurking and the eavesdropping and the pathetic pining. What was happening to him? Rachel had no interest in him beyond the fact that he was Annie and Abby's father, and that's exactly how it should be. She was an employee—not his confidante, not his lover and certainly not his soul mate. Ian wasn't even sure he believed in the concept of soul mates anymore. As much as he'd loved Serena, their relationship had never been the head-over-heels, all-consuming type of love. He'd never lost control and done something as stupid as hide in a hallway and spy on her, and that had suited Ian just fine. When he'd lost her, he'd still been devastated. How much worse would it have been if he'd truly been wrapped up in his feelings for her, enough to lose his head?

He preferred being in control of his emotions, more so now than ever before. His girls needed him to be strong, stable and consistent. Always holding himself together enough to put them first. The more control he had over his head, his heart and his home, the better.

"Ian. Um, good morning." Rachel's eyes grew wide as she peered at him over the top of one of Elma's famous cinnamon rolls.

He met her gaze head on. *Yes, I heard every word*

you just said, and I'm fine with it. So totally fine that his jaw seemed to be clenching of its own volition.

Her lips parted ever so slightly, almost like she wanted to explain herself but didn't dare.

Ian stared for a beat, drawn in by the sight of her pink-carnation mouth. So lush, so perfect.

So utterly out of his reach. Period.

"Good morning, Elma." Ian turned toward his mother-in-law and gave her a hug. "I hope you had a nice trip."

Elma let out a tiny gasp, as if the embrace had caught her by surprise, which only made Ian feel worse. Had he really been that standoffish toward her recently?

Probably. But now Rachel was here, helping to thaw things between them, working the same strange and special magic on everyone that had already completely enamored his girls.

Panic clawed at his insides. What the hell was he going to do when she left? And why, oh why, couldn't she stay?

"Asheville was lovely," Elma said, wiping down the kitchen counter even though it was already spotless. Ordinarily, such a move would've irritated Ian to no end. Now he recognized it as a product of nervous energy. Perhaps he wasn't the only one who craved the sense of being in control. "I bought an antique dollhouse for the girls. I thought maybe I could help them decorate it."

He nodded. "That sounds nice. I'm sure they'll love it."

Elma handed him a plate with not just one but two fragrant cinnamon rolls on it. "It's in the trunk of my car. Maybe you can bring it in after you eat."

So much for his morning run.

"I'd be happy to go get it," Rachel said, grabbing Elma's keys off the kitchen counter and making herself scarce before either of them could stop her.

Always so eager to run away. Bitterness churned Ian's stomach. He was being unfair and he knew it. When had he turned into such a complete and total jerk?

He sat down at the kitchen table and plunged a fork into a gooey, warm roll while Elma took a seat across from him. She made a point of glancing out the window toward the carriage house and then directly back at him, eyes blazing. Elma and Rachel might have reached a tentative understanding, but clearly, the jury was still out on whether there would be any forgiveness for Ian.

"Elma." He put his fork down and folded his hands, doing his best to sound calm and reasonable, even though inside he felt anything but. Rachel's voice kept repeating over and over again in his head on a loop.

There's nothing between Ian and me.

"As I'm sure you know by now, I've hired Rachel as the twins' new nanny. She's staying in the carriage house." He cleared his throat. "For now."

"So I've heard." Elma sniffed.

Ian desperately wanted to remind her that had she not let herself into his home in the early, predawn hours with no warning whatsoever, she never would've been caught so off guard by Rachel's presence. Now didn't seem like the time.

"She's great with the girls, and I know you want what's best for them just as much as I do," he said.

"Yes, but—"

He held up a hand, gently cutting her off. "But the carriage house will still be there for you when the time is right. Serena made you a promise, and of course I'm going to honor it."

Elma pursed her lips, unconvinced.

Ian sighed. "Rachel was living in the residence hotel downtown. Would you really have me leave her there?" He hadn't actually realized she'd been living there when he'd first made the offer—but Elma didn't need to know that.

Elma dropped her gaze to the tablecloth. "I suppose that's really no place for a nice young woman to live on a long-term basis."

"That's what I thought too. I was simply trying to do the right thing," Ian said, but the great unspoken thing was still there, as real as if it had pulled up a chair and helped itself to the food on Ian's plate.

The cinnamon roll felt like it was rotting in the pit of his stomach. "There's nothing going on between me and Rachel," he somehow managed to say.

It wasn't a lie, but it sure as heck felt like one—especially when he looked up to find Rachel standing in the doorway with an enormous antique dollhouse in her arms. He could have sworn he saw a flicker of hurt in her emerald eyes, but that wasn't possible. He'd simply been echoing her sentiments.

"Let me help you with that." Ian scrambled to his feet.

The vintage dollhouse was a fanciful pink Victorian, with gingerbread trim and a roof covered in miniature gray shingles. It had a white picket fence and a turret, like something out of a fairy tale, but Ian's gaze snagged on the tiny railed platform that extended from the overlapping shingles on the upper story. A "widow's walk," as it was more commonly known.

Widow.

That's what Ian was now, wasn't he? A widower. He was usually so busy dealing with the girls and trying to grapple with what the loss meant to them that he didn't think much about his marital status. But every so often, the fact of the matter hit him like a ton of bricks.

He was a widower, or as they said in ancient times, a relic—literally a leftover person.

"I can get it," he said, tightening his grip on the dollhouse. But his voice sounded raw and vulnerable, even to his own ears.

Rachel followed his gaze to the miniature widow's walk, and the flash of hurt in her eyes morphed quickly into something else. Something far worse.

Pity.

That was the last thing Ian wanted from Rachel. He might be conflicted about what exactly he *did* want, but he knew for certain it wasn't pity.

"Rachel," he said, swallowing hard. "Please."

Her eyes seemed to plead with him, and for once, he was grateful for Elma's presence. He wouldn't… *couldn't*…talk to Rachel about what it felt like being the leftover half of a whole that no longer existed. If he opened that forbidden Pandora's box of feelings, he'd have to lift the lid all the way and let everything out. And she wouldn't want to hear the ugly truth— the guilt that wound its way through him, knowing that the girls might have been better off with their mother as a solo parent instead of their father. The way he leaned into mental and emotional numbness because it protected him from feelings he'd rather not experience full force. But most of all, if he was truly open with her, he'd reveal the way he'd begun to slowly come to life again the more time he spent in Rachel's presence.

It was as wrong as it was ridiculous, but he was developing feelings for her—feelings that he now knew with absolute certainty were only one-sided. And he was going to have to come up with a better way to hide them, sooner rather than later.

Ian tugged on the dollhouse. Were they really going to stand there in a literal and metaphorical tug-of-war over a picture-perfect home, complete with mom and dad, two kids and a white picket fence?

"It's all yours," Rachel finally said. "If that's what you want."

Then she let go, shifting the burden solely into Ian's grasp as Elma looked on, oblivious to all that had just transpired.

Ian hoped so, anyway.

Chapter Seven

"I want kitties!" Abby peered up and down the row of dog kennels at the Furever Paws shelter the following afternoon, clearly unimpressed with the canine shelter residents. "Miss Rachel promised kitties. I want them."

Rachel bent down so they were eye to eye while a shaggy white dog peered at them from behind a mop of fur in a nearby kennel. "I did say we'd see kitties, but do you remember what else I said?"

"Pet dogs too." Abby heaved a sigh that seemed to far outweigh her tiny body. "Please. I *need* kitties."

Ian ruffled her hair. "Wait your turn, pumpkin. Your sister is still visiting the dogs."

"We've been here thirty hundred hours," Abby said.

They had, in fact, been at Furever Paws for less than a quarter hour. Rachel was keeping track, because Ian had promised the girls thirty minutes with the dogs and thirty minutes with the cats. In the interest of fairness, he'd flipped a coin to determine which kennel area they'd visit first—heads for cats and tails for dogs, which in itself caused a bit of confusion because cats and dogs both have tails. But the dogs had won fair and square.

"Only thirty hundred more to go." Ian winked, and the tiny gesture seemed to float through Rachel on butterfly wings.

He's not flirting. He's being sweet to his daughter, not *you.*

At least, that's what Rachel could only assume. Things had been rather stilted between them since Elma's return. Rachel wasn't completely sure why, but a stone had settled in the pit of her stomach when he'd strolled into the kitchen right on the heels of her promise that her stay in Spring Forest was only temporary. That stone hadn't budged.

She kept telling herself that she had nothing to feel guilty about. Rachel had been completely upfront and honest when Ian offered her the nanny job. She had no intention of staying in their picturesque small town. It was far too risky.

Even so, the way he'd looked at her—like one

of the homeless dogs in the shelter—had just about ripped her in two.

Space…distance…that's what they needed. They needed to stop acting like a cozy little family and re-establish some professional boundaries for the sake of the twins.

For the sake of my heart.

Rachel swallowed and redirected her gaze from Ian's chiseled face to Annie, who was petting a beautiful golden retriever puppy through the chain-link gate to its kennel.

"Hi, Miss Dog," Annie whispered.

The puppy's golden ears swiveled back and forth.

"This sweet little girl is named Pancake," a woman with gorgeous hair, a thick fringe of bangs and wearing a Furever Paws staff T-shirt said. She shifted a giant bag of dog food from one arm to the other as she paused to smile down at Annie petting the dog. "Hi, I'm Bethany, the shelter director."

Annie rubbed the dog's soft ear between her fingertips, much like she often did to her favorite blanket at home, but said nothing.

Ian finally filled the silence. "Hello. Ian Parsons. Nice to meet you. These are my girls, Annie and Abby, and this is Rachel, our nanny and…family friend."

"Nice to meet you all. Is your family looking for a pet?" Bethany glanced at Pancake and gave a little wince. "Because I'm afraid Pancake isn't ready for a forever home quite yet."

Too bad. She seemed almost as shy as Annie and every bit as sweet. Rachel thought they might help each other.

But Ian had made it clear they were just visiting today. Adopting a pet certainly wasn't the sort of decision that should be made by the nanny.

Rachel bent down to run her fingers over the pup's soft fur. "She's awfully cute. Is she okay?"

"We've just learned that she has a heart murmur, so we've got to get her evaluated and determine when she can be safely spayed. Until then, I'm afraid she needs to stay here." Bethany sighed. "Pancake was actually adopted out a while ago, before we found out about the heart murmur, but she was returned to the shelter because her pet parent thought she was too shy."

Rachel sensed Ian stiffening beside her.

"That's terrible," he said.

Bethany nodded. "I agree, but unfortunately, things like that happen. We'll make sure she finds the right family—someplace where she can really shine."

Ian cleared his throat, and his gaze shifted to Annie.

Rachel had to stop herself from tucking her arm through his and telling him that Annie was going to be just fine. *More* than fine. He was a good dad, and Annie was already in the perfect home. With love and care—and most especially time—she'd shine, too, just like Pancake.

"We have a lot of other wonderful dogs, though." Bethany waved a free hand toward the row of kennels where hopeful dog noses poked through the chain-link gates. Annie had already stopped to personally greet at least ten of them. "And Pancake is comfortable and happy and will be cared for, no matter the outcome of her vet evaluation. You have my word."

"Daddy, the kitties." Abby tugged on Ian's pant leg. "You *promised.*"

Rachel glanced at the time on her phone. Uh-oh, puppy time was up, and they'd only made it through half the dog kennel area. "Just like clockwork. It's time to switch."

Bethany nodded toward the end of the hall. "The cattery is that way. Enjoy, and if you need any help or want more information about one of the animals, I'll be up front in the lobby, and there are other volunteers around."

"Thank you." Ian gestured to the dog food in her arms. "Can I give you a hand with that?"

Bethany laughed. "Oh, I'm used to it. Believe me."

She turned to go, and the dogs all pranced toward the front of their kennels to wag goodbye as she passed.

Ian crouched down and tapped Annie gently on the tip of her nose. "What do you say, kiddo? Are you ready to go visit the cats with your sister?"

Pancake's little head bobbed up and down as the puppy did a few long blinks.

"I think Pancake might be ready for a nap," Rachel said.

"Pancake go night night," Annie whispered and then scrambled to her feet to hold Rachel's hand.

"That's right. We'll let her get some rest while we go see the kitties." Rachel ran her thumb along Annie's soft little knuckles.

"Kitties! *Finally.*" Abby began dragging Ian toward the cattery.

He cast Rachel a glance over his shoulder and mouthed *help me*. But Rachel wasn't fooled. He was enjoying himself every bit as much as the girls were, and if he wasn't careful, the pitter-patter of little feet in the Parsons household might soon include a new set of paws.

Just what Rachel needed—another warm body to get attached to, right here in Spring Forest. But somehow she didn't mind much, especially when she made eye contact with a big black dog nestled in the back corner of his kennel as she rounded the corner toward the cattery. Rachel knew that hollow, empty look in the pup's eyes. She knew what it felt like to need a soft place to land, a place to call home. She remembered the feeling all too well, and living with Ian, Abby and Annie had changed everything. Sometimes, when she let her guard slip, it felt like she was closing her eyes and sinking into a feather bed—warm, comforting and downy soft.

For as long as it lasted, anyway.

"I'm beginning to understand why the expression *herding cats* is a thing." Ian frowned as a tiny gray kitten darted past his right foot at the same moment that a pair of skinny black-and-white tuxedo cats rolled between his legs in a tangled ball of fur and whiskers.

He'd gotten off work early Tuesday afternoon so he could visit the animal shelter with Rachel and the girls, as promised. It didn't take a crystal ball to know within seconds of darkening the door of Furever Paws that he was in trouble.

Had he really thought he could take two toddlers to visit a pet rescue operation and go home empty-handed?

"Abby, honey. Why don't we sit down and see if a kitten might crawl into your lap?" Rachel reached to take one of Abby's tiny hands in hers, but she was too slow.

Sitting still didn't seem at all likely, considering

Abby was so thrilled to be surrounded by cats that she was bouncing off the walls. Clearly, an animal wasn't going to help their efforts to get Abby to calm down a bit. At the moment, Abby was in hot pursuit of an orange cat with a bent tail she was convinced might be Oliver.

It wasn't, unfortunately. Ian had seen so many posters of Oliver's ginger face that he would know that cat anywhere. Plus he wholeheartedly doubted that Birdie and Bunny Whitaker—the sisters who owned Furever Paws and the surrounding property, known as Whitaker Acres—would ever harbor a feline fugitive, particularly when his sweet owner missed her cat so desperately. Nor would Oliver have slipped under the radar, undetected.

The Whitaker sisters were Spring Forest's resident animal saviors and the founders of Furever Paws. With all the posters around town, they would have recognized Oliver in an instant. A stray dog or cat couldn't set paw within the town limits without Birdie or Bunny swooping in to rescue the poor thing. Most recently, the sisters had helped find temporary homes for a huge number of dogs and cats that had been seized from an unscrupulous backyard breeder by the North Carolina ASPCA. They'd taken in several of the dogs and one of the cats themselves, finding room for the neglected animals at Furever

Paws and with foster families throughout the community.

No wonder he could barely take a step without narrowly missing a kitten.

"Olly-ver!" Abby cried and darted toward a peach-colored ball of fluff, before getting distracted by a calico kitten batting a felt mouse across the floor. "Olly-ver, Olly-ver, Olly-ver."

"Is it possible she thinks they're all Oliver?" Ian glanced at Rachel and laughed as Abby plowed into his knees.

Before he could gather his daughter into his arms, she was off again, running back and forth the length of the screened-in porch where the feline residents of the shelter were allowed to roam free and get fresh air. Fortunately, the kittens seemed to think it was a game. The older cats were all perched atop elevated scratching posts and cat trees, safely out of reach and watching with obvious feline disdain.

"She seems a little excited," Rachel said, biting back a smile.

"You think?" Ian laughed, vaguely aware his favorite suit was currently covered in cat hair. Somehow it didn't seem to bother him all that much. That's what dry cleaners were for.

Ian hadn't seen his girls so full of joy in a long, long time. While Abby chased kittens to and fro, Annie stared longingly out the window at a hand-

ful of the shelter's canine residents being walked
by volunteers. She giggled and waved at each dog
that passed by, earning tail wags and happy doggy
grins in return.

Ian's heart clenched. He couldn't remember the
last time he'd heard his quiet little girl laugh like
that.

"I'm pretty sure Abby's using Oliver's name in-
terchangeably with the word *cat* now." Rachel shot
him a sheepish grin. "You can fire me anytime you
like. Clearly, I'm doing a stellar job."

"Not a chance," Ian said before he could stop
himself.

For a second or two, the awkwardness between
them melted away. Since Elma's surprise visit yesterday morning and their mutual insistence that
nothing romantic was developing between them,
Ian had gotten the sense that he and Rachel had
both been walking on eggshells. And now, with kittens running amok and the sound of his children's
laughter echoing off the shelter's soothing gray-blue
walls, the conversation with Elma didn't seem quite
as important.

Had he been completely honest with his mother-
in-law? Had Rachel?

Ian didn't know. He didn't know much of anything, it seemed…

Except that being here, surrounded by all the homeless animals, made him want to adopt a pet.

Rachel looked away, the sudden softness in her eyes vanishing. Back to awkward in three, two...

"Ian Parsons, is that you? We heard you and your sweet girls were here."

Ian turned around to find Bunny Whitaker herself standing just inside the entrance to the cattery. A slim gentleman with salt-and-pepper hair stood just behind her, and each of them carried a tiny kitten in each hand.

"Bunny, hello." Ian laughed. "It certainly looks like you two have your hands full."

"Says the father of twin toddlers." Bunny shot him a comically exaggerated eye-roll and set the kittens down in a nearby crate.

The man added his two kittens to the mix and then held out his hand. "Hi, there. I'm Stew, Bunny's—"

"Friend," Bunny blurted before Stew could get another word out.

Ian held back a laugh. Clearly, there was more going on there than simple friendship. He knew the story, of course. The whole town had followed the saga like it was some kind of soap opera on TV. Bunny, who had been single for many years after losing her fiancé in a tragic accident when she was in her twenties, had met Stew online and they'd had a secret romance. Well, secret until he'd shown up in a camper van and swept her off her feet the previous year. They'd run off together into the sunset... up until Bunny had come back, *alone*, a few months earlier. No one knew quite what had happened—but when Stew had followed after, still just as clearly committed to Bunny as ever, the town had all but broken out bags of popcorn to watch the show.

Ian tried not to get involved in gossip, but in his own way, he was rooting for the couple. He hoped they'd figure out their way to happiness together, despite all the complications. He liked a good love story. As long as it wasn't his own.

Because there's nothing happening between you and Rachel. She's the twins' nanny, full stop.

Maybe if he kept telling himself that, he'd eventually believe it.

"It's a pleasure to meet you, Stew. This is Rachel, and these are my girls, Annie and Abby." Ian waved a hand toward Annie, still glued to the window, watching the dogs, and Abby, who let out a piercing giggle as a cat rubbed against her legs.

"Hi." Rachel held up her hand in greeting.

"Can I help you with anything before I put Stew to work bathing puppies?" Bunny asked.

Stew blinked. "I'm bathing puppies?"

"Yes. What did you think I meant when I told you to brace yourself to get down and dirty?"

Stew's face flamed beet red while Bunny kept

looking at him, wide-eyed and charmingly oblivious. "Um."

"We're good here," Ian said.

"You're sure?" Bunny said.

"Yes," Ian and Rachel said in unison. Ian didn't
dare look at her, for fear their composure might
crack and they'd both start laughing. He'd never
want to hurt Bunny's feelings.

"Okay, then. We're off to get dirty." Bunny nodded. "Come on, Stew."

Stew shrugged and fell in step behind her.

"Wow, that was—" Rachel's lips twitched
"—something."

"Bunny's a character. She and her sister are pet
rescue superheroes." Ian twirled a finger to encompass the general surroundings. "They own this entire piece of land and have basically dedicated all
the nearby acreage, along with their lives, to animal
rescue."

"Really?" Rachel's eyes glittered with wonder.
"That's amazing."

"They could probably track down a rescue pig if
you're interested." Ian shrugged one of his muscular shoulders. "Or a llama."

"I think I'll pass on the livestock." Rachel's gaze
narrowed. "But can I ask you a question?"

"I'm an open book," Ian said.

Liar, he immediately thought. His heart had

slammed shut when Serena died, and he only let it creak open for his daughters.

Until lately.

Rachel tilted her head and appraised him up and down. "Which do you prefer—cats or dogs?"

"Neither. I suppose I have a soft spot for anyone and anything that makes my girls smile, regardless of species. Dog. Cat. Teacup pig. I just want them to be happy." Was it weird to admit that? Being around Rachel made him introspective about a lot of things. He felt about as secure as a teenager who longed to ask a girl to prom.

"That's incredibly sweet." Rachel's lovely mouth curved into a grin so wide that dimples flashed in her cheeks.

Their gazes met and held, until Rachel cleared her throat, crossed her arms and looked away.

"Daddy, look. Olly-ver likes me." Abby clapped her hands to her cheeks as a cat who looked nothing whatsoever like the missing Oliver batted a paw at one of her shoelaces.

Ian took a deep breath. Was he really going to do this?

"Do you mind keeping an eye on the girls while I go talk to the shelter manager and find out what she needs from me in order to eventually become a pet parent?" He bent to quietly whisper the question in Rachel's ear.

"Are you serious?" She tilted her head and searched his gaze as her cheeks went cotton candy pink.

Ian had to remind himself he was inquiring about bringing a pet home to make his kids happy, not just so his nanny would look at him the way Rachel was right now—with a softness in her eyes that made his chest ache.

He swallowed hard. "Not today...but soon. Maybe? You're the one who said I needed to open myself up to new experiences. Set a good example for the girls."

Rachel beamed at him. "I think that's a marvelous idea."

"Are you absolutely sure? Because, unfortunately, you're going to be the one stuck at home with two kids and a fur ball while I'm at work." He grinned, until a nagging detail he couldn't seem to forget reared its ugly head. "Temporarily, of course."

She blinked, and her wide smile seemed to freeze into place. "Right. Of course."

This isn't forever. They weren't a real family, no matter how much they were beginning to feel like one.

Ian suddenly wanted to get out of there. He needed air, like one of the sad little cats or dogs that didn't have a place, or a *person*, to call home.

"So," he said, apropos of nothing.

"So."

Why couldn't he seem to talk to her anymore? He should have never eavesdropped on her conversation with Elma. Or rather, he shouldn't have had such an extreme reaction to what he'd heard. Nothing Rachel had said to Elma should have been breaking news, but it had taken him by surprise all the same.

He could have sworn he'd felt the faint stirring of something developing between them. He hadn't dared to put a label on it, but he'd felt it, and he'd been certain Rachel had too. Perhaps it really had been just one-sided. Perhaps he'd simply mistaken friendship for something else.

Perhaps he needed to focus all his energy on his family and stop letting himself get derailed by feelings he should have never been having in the first place.

Ian nodded in the direction of the shelter lobby. "I'm going to go find Bethany. I'll be back in a few minutes."

"We'll be right here," Rachel said.

Ian ruffled Annie's hair as he headed out of the cattery, and she let out a soft woof. Ever so slowly, his shy daughter was coming out of her shell. Ian just hoped she wouldn't close herself up in it again once Rachel decided to move on.

He was starting to wonder if bringing someone so intimately into their home life had been such a good idea. It had sure seemed like one at the time, and so far, Annie and Abby had both been improving by leaps and bounds. He just hadn't given any thought to what might happen once Rachel's state accreditation came through and she started to look for a new job.

And he wasn't going to think about it now, either. They were having a good day—maybe even a *great* day—and he didn't want to spoil it.

"Can I help you, Ian?" Bethany looked up at Ian from beneath her fringe of caramel-colored bangs as he approached the reception area.

"I think so." Ian took a deep breath. Was he really ready for this? "I'm interested in learning more about the adoption process."

Bethany exchanged a quick glance with the shelter volunteer sitting beside her, eyes twinkling. "Excellent. Is there a particular pet you're interested in? As I'm sure you can see, we've got plenty to choose from."

"Not yet. For now, I just wanted to know how to go about it or possibly get preapproved?"

"Like you would for a home mortgage?" Bethany's mouth quirked into a grin. "Or a car loan?"

Ian winced. Sometimes, it was hard to turn off his engineering brain, but he was working on it. "Let me guess. Adopting an animal doesn't work that way?"

"Nope. I'm afraid not." Bethany shook her head.

"It's not really something you can prep for in advance. You're not going to know what you need just from filling out a form. It's all about chemistry—finding the one that's meant to be with you. If you need help matching with a particular animal, we can certainly give you some help. We like to make sure potential adopters find just the right pet. It's in the best interest for both the adoptive family and the animal."

He nodded. "Completely understandable. I'm just not sure where to begin, I guess."

Bethany stood, a woman on a mission. "We're here to help. First question—cat or dog?"

"That's precisely the problem. One of my twins loves cats and the other loves dogs."

Bethany's eyebrows drew together. "I see. That's a quandary, isn't it? Unless…"

Of course Bunny and Stew chose that precise moment to stroll toward the front desk from the staff offices, wearing vinyl aprons splashed with colorful letters that spelled out Bath Time Doesn't Have to Be Ruff. Ian was about to get tag-teamed, and he definitely had a feeling he wouldn't stand a chance against a single Whitaker sister and her animal-saving entourage.

"Sometimes two is better than one. You should know that, Ian," Bunny said with a wink.

Ian held up a hand. He'd never had any pets before. No way was he starting off by adopting one of each.

No.

Possible.

Way.

Before he could say so, though, Rachel came flying into the lobby from the direction of the cattery, looking as white and pale as the alabaster kitten named Snowball they'd met earlier. She was carrying Abby in her arms, and the little girl appeared equally upset, with tears brimming in her big blue eyes.

Dread shot through Ian's system, hard and fast. Something was very, very wrong.

Then Rachel spoke, and the dread coursing through Ian's body crystallized into something far worse—stone-cold fear.

"Annie's gone missing."

Chapter Eight

This can't be happening.

Rachel gulped air into her lungs. Was she hyperventilating? She wasn't sure, as she'd never hyperventilated before. But losing someone's child seemed like the perfect occasion to start.

"Daddy?" Abby's little voice went wobbly, and Rachel longed for a paper bag to breathe into. "Where's Annie?"

Marvelous. Rachel had not only lost sight of Ian's quiet daughter, but in her panic, she'd managed to frighten his more confident one into sounding more timid than she ever had before. She should be tossed straight into nanny jail.

"It's going to be fine, sweetheart. We'll find her," Ian said, eerily calm as he reached for Abby.

She shifted from Rachel's arms into Ian's, and Rachel instantly felt untethered. Lost. Just like Annie.

"I'm so sorry." Rachel wrapped her arms around herself. "She was right there, watching the dogs out the window."

Until she wasn't...

"It's my fault. I shouldn't have left you there alone with two toddlers and all those kittens." Ian shook his head, gaze flitting around the lobby. As calm as he seemed, Rachel could tell he was as equally alarmed as she was. He was just better at hiding it—solid dad skills. "Don't worry. She's got to be around here somewhere."

Bethany came out from behind the reception desk. She held up her hands. "We'll find her. The only way in and out of this shelter is through the front door. I would have seen her if she passed through here alone anytime in the past half hour."

"She's not in the staff office area. We just came from there," Bunny said, offering Rachel a sympathetic smile. "Don't worry, dear. With all of us looking for her, she'll turn up right away."

"It's only been a minute or so since she disappeared. Maybe not even that long. I glanced around, and when I didn't see her in the cattery, the exercise yard or the hallway, I came straight here." Rachel swallowed. She felt like she'd lived and died in the course of sixty seconds or less.

"Okay. I think we should split up and search the entire building," Bethany said. She glanced at the volunteer who'd been manning the reception desk alongside her—a woman in a Furever Paws T-shirt wearing a name tag that said "Woof, my name's Amanda." "Can you please keep an eye out for Annie while we take a look around?"

"Absolutely. I won't budge from the desk." Amanda crossed her heart. "If I see her, we'll make an announcement over the intercom system and also come and find one of you."

"Perfect." Bethany nodded, cool as a cucumber. She and Bunny probably had loads of experience tracking down missing dogs and cats, right? Rachel prayed that was the case. She was ready to grab on to every last bit of hope she could find.

"Now, do you have any idea where Annie might have gone?" Bunny asked.

"Annie loves dogs," Rachel said, voice trembling beyond her control. Abby's bottom lip began to quiver, so she reached out to pat the little girl's shoulder.

"Perfect. Why don't the two of you go check the dog kennels, and I'll take a look in the visitation rooms and the exercise yard?" Bethany waved a hand toward the long hallway behind the lobby, the only way out of the room, save for the gift shop off to the side. "Bunny and Stew can check out the veterinary clinic area. We'll catch up to you afterward, and if we still haven't found her, we'll start again in the cattery."

"Got it," Ian nodded.

He turned toward Rachel, and her stomach plummeted. She bit down hard on the inside of her cheek to keep her teeth from chattering as she braced herself to be yelled at.

Or worse.

But Ian simply took her by the hand and tugged her closer to him. "Let's go find her."

Tears stung the backs of her eyes, and she wasn't even sure why…except she'd never been treated with such kindness in the wake of making a mistake before. Just the prospect of disappointing someone made her panicky.

Old habits die hard and so do old expectations, even in the presence of a good man like Ian.

Rachel had been doing so well here in Spring Forest. She'd felt so safe, and all it had taken was a sliver of a moment to catapult her back into feeling absolutely worthless. How had she let this happen?

"Hey." Ian glanced at her and squeezed her hand tight as they stalked down the hall toward the dog kennels. "Are you okay? You're not going to faint on me, are you?"

"We just need to find her," Rachel said. "I'll be fine once we find her." Once they'd located Annie, she could curl into a ball and cry her eyes out. Until then, she at least needed to stay upright. In this moment, Abby and Ian shouldn't have to worry about her too.

Ian kept a death grip on her hand until they reached the rows of dog kennels at the end of the hall. Only then did he give her fingertips one last squeeze and let go. "I'll take the right and you take the left?"

Rachel nodded, not quite trusting herself to speak. The lump in her throat kept getting bigger and bigger.

And then Ian was gone, peering into kennels as he went. Abby's slender arms were wrapped around his neck, and she was still hoisted into his arms as if she weighed no more than a tiny puppy. Rachel took a deep breath and turned in the opposite direction.

"Annie?" she called, over and over again. "Honey, are you here somewhere?"

She passed a kennel holding a happy little spaniel who poked her nose through the gate to try and lick Rachel's hand. Next, a poodle mix greeted her with a chorus of yips as she twirled in circles. One by one, the dogs wagged their tails as she peered inside their kennels, but Annie was nowhere to be found.

Then Rachel reached the kennel at the very end of the row. This time, there was no dog standing just on the other side of the gate to welcome her with a bark or a swipe of a pink tongue. And when Rachel looked closer, she realized the gate wasn't latched.

Heart pounding hard, she crouched down and squinted through the chain link. A sob nearly escaped her when her gaze landed on Annie, sleeping soundly on a dog bed near the back of the kennel with her head nestled against a glossy black Labrador retriever with sweet chocolate eyes—the same sad dog Rachel had seen earlier. The only one that hadn't seemed at all interested in socializing.

Oh, thank goodness.

Rachel could have cried with relief. When she called out to the others, her voice broke. "I found her, everyone! We're back here." She glanced at the nameplate hanging on the gate of the kennel. "At Pepper and Salty's crate!"

Weird. Rachel hadn't noticed a second dog in the kennel—just the sweet black Lab, who suddenly didn't seem to want to leave Annie's side.

"Annie, honey. Wake up, sweetheart. We've all been looking for you," Rachel said, opening the gate so she could make her way inside the kennel.

And then a wholly unexpected sound stopped her in her tracks.

Meow.

Rachel looked around. Was she hearing things? Dogs didn't meow. She stared at the Lab—Pepper, she presumed, if the color of her coat was any indication. "That wasn't you, was it?"

The dog opened her mouth and let out a squeaky dog yawn just as another wailing meow came seemingly out of nowhere. Annie's eyes fluttered open, and she sat up. Pepper planted her big black head in the toddler's lap, staking her claim. She didn't seem in the slightest bit concerned by the cat noises coming out of nowhere.

"Annie!" Ian skidded to a stop in front of the kennel and set Abby down gently on the floor.

Bunny and Stew arrived from the other direction, right on their heels.

"Daddy," Annie said, rubbing her eyes before throwing her arms around the black pup's neck. "My new doggy friend!"

Ian's eyes went shiny, and Rachel wasn't sure if it was because Annie sounded so cheery and confident or because she'd been found. If she'd had to guess, she would have said both in equal parts.

"I see, sweetheart," he said. Then quieter, at barely more than a whisper, he added, "You gave us all a scare for a few minutes there."

Another meow came from the back of the kennel, and suddenly, a distinctly feline head popped up from behind Pepper and Annie's cuddly lovefest.

"Olly-ver!" Abby squealed, and then she pushed open the gate and skipped into the kennel.

When she fell to her knees in front of Pepper, the cat tiptoed his way out from behind the dog. Bright blue eyes shone from his dark face. Fawn-colored fur, offset by his dark legs and tail, made him immediately recognizable as a Siamese kitty.

"Pretty," Abby said in a voice brimming with awe.

She held out her hand, and the cat rubbed his face against Abby's pudgy fingers.

"Wow," Rachel murmured and felt herself smile for the first time since Annie had gone missing.

"I can't quite believe what I'm seeing right now," Bethany said.

Rachel had been so caught up in watching the twins with the dog and cat that Bethany's arrival on the scene hadn't even registered.

"Huh." Bunny's brows knitted. "That *is* Pepper and Salty, right?"

Bethany nodded without taking her eyes off Abby, Annie and the sweet animals. "Yep."

"I don't understand. Are the dog and cat not supposed to be in the kennel together? Are they not safe with kids?" Ian said, a flash of concern creeping into the relief in his gaze.

"Oh, they definitely are. Pepper and Salty were rescued together from a backyard breeder. They were the owner's pets. The poor things are inseparable. They're harmless, but just so bonded with each other that they don't really like people. I'm the only one that either one of them seems to tolerate. It's why we've had trouble getting them adopted. Well, that and the fact that it's tricky to find someone who wants a dog *and* a cat, and we couldn't bear the thought of separating them." Bethany's eyes flickered with wonder…and more than a little bit of hope. "Until now."

Salty, the cat, stretched to lick Abby's face, and instead of collapsing into giggles or getting overexcited, Abby stroked his fur in soft, careful movements, while Annie kept her little arms anchored around Pepper's neck.

"Well, would you look at that?" Bunny crossed her arms, tilted her head and aimed a questioning glance at Ian.

Rachel's gaze slid toward him, too, with joy dancing in her heart. Pepper and Salty were perfect, and just one look at Ian told her he felt the same.

Ian Parsons was about to be the dad of yet another twosome.

Ian was going to need a bigger car. A bigger mudroom. Possibly a bigger house altogether.

"What have I done?" he said under his breath as he finished assembling the massive crate he'd purchased on the way home from the Furever Paws shelter.

He stood to get a good look at the monstrosity that was now taking up over half the square footage of the mudroom.

"You've made your little girls ridiculously happy." Rachel nodded toward the living room, where Annie, Abby, Pepper and Salty were all piled on the floor together watching *Lady and the Tramp*. The dog was snoring loud enough to peel the paint off the walls, and every time one of the girls dropped a piece of popcorn, the cat batted at it with his paws. "*That's* what you've done."

It was an idyllic scene, to be sure. But Ian was still reeling a bit from the extensive list of instructions Bethany had handed him after he'd managed to get both of the twins and the animals settled inside his modest-sized SUV. Not to mention the shopping list...

While Rachel had gotten the kids and the new pets settled at home, Ian had made a trip to the local pet shop and purchased everything the dog and cat might need—starting with a crate that seemed big enough for a small elephant.

He crossed his arms and assessed its bulk. "I

think there's enough room for Annie and Abby in here, along with Salty and Pepper."

Rachel held a finger up to her lips. "You'd better not give them any ideas."

He laughed. "Point taken."

"Bethany said Salty and Pepper are used to sleeping together. It's probably a good idea to get them used to their new home in a safe, secure area like a crate before you try letting them sleep loose in the house." Rachel dropped to her hands and knees to arrange a soft bed with a bolster around the edges—another new purchase—inside the crate.

"True. I think I might have overdone it on the size of this thing, though." Ian laughed.

Rachel sat back on her heels. "Better too big than too small, though, right?"

She had a point, but before Ian could tell her so, the knob on the back door started to rattle.

"Uh-oh." Rachel's eyes went wide. "Is that—"

Yes…yes, it was.

Elma swung the door open, once again wielding her emergency key.

"Elma." Ian scurried to stand in front of the crate, as if hiding such a behemoth was remotely possible. "Nice to see you."

He was being ridiculous. He was a grown man—this was his home, his life. He'd done nothing wrong whatsoever, and he wasn't required to justify any of his decisions, especially when it came to his daughters.

But dealing with Elma was never easy. Since Serena's death, she saw any and all forms of change in their lives as a threat—as if they were taking another step away from Serena. As difficult as she could be, Ian's heart went out to his mother-in-law. He just really wished she'd stop turning up out of the blue and surprising him before he had a chance to give her his family's major life updates.

"Nice to see you too," Elma said as she lingered in the kitchen, clutching one of her casserole dishes covered in plastic wrap.

Chicken tetrazzini. Ian could smell it from the mudroom.

He wasn't about to complain. The fact that Elma seemed so pleasantly surprised by his effusive greeting made his gut churn with shame. Was he really ordinarily so cranky that the simplest of kind words would stop her in her tracks?

He hated to admit it, but yes. Until recently, at least. He'd been feeling more and more like his old self lately. Whole…almost.

Elma's forehead crinkled and she blinked as she took in the sight of the giant dog crate looming behind Ian. "Is that a *cage*? For your *children*?"

Rachel held up her hands. "Goodness, no. Of course not."

Ian's stomach roiled, and not just from the thought of chicken tetrazzini. Surely his mother-in-law didn't think he'd put his daughters in an animal crate. Although, in her defense, it was definitely large enough to house a few toddlers.

"Actually," he said, and before he could manage to utter another syllable, Salty sprang out of nowhere, landing on the kitchen counter immediately to Elma's left with a bellowing meow.

She screamed and the casserole dish went crashing to the ground. "Ahhh!"

Salty hopped down from the counter and began licking delicately at the mess of chicken and noodles. Pepper trotted into the kitchen and joined him, slurping at the spaghetti with loud, smacking noises as Elma's mouth dropped open in abject horror.

Rachel made a valiant attempt at jazz hands. "Surprise."

Chapter Nine

Ian couldn't sleep. He'd been staring at the ceiling for over an hour as his disaster of an evening played over and over in his mind, like a bad dream.

Elma had been livid. He made a mental note to buy her a new casserole dish, given that her favorite one had cracked in two when it hit the floor. Of course, he could buy her a dish in solid gold and Ian doubted it would be enough to make her forget the sight of her chicken tetrazzini all over the kitchen tile. Or Pepper staring up at her with a long noodle draped over her nose. Or the way the girls had giggled over her indignation every time Salty got anywhere near her for the rest of the night. Appeasing Elma was worth a try, though, even if it was a long shot.

But things hadn't been *all* bad. The more Ian lay there in the dark, the more his thoughts seemed to gravitate toward the little snippets of joy that had taken place that evening—the delicious taste of takeout burgers with homemade root beer from the Main Street Grille, the warm weight of Pepper's body as she'd curled on top of Ian's feet under the dinner table, Rachel and her penchant for jazz hands.

But Ian's favorite memories from the evening were the sounds of Annie's and Abby's laughter, ringing through the house like church bells. Once, when Ian was a little boy, his grandmother had told him that in ancient times Christians believed the ringing of bells drove out demons. At the time, the sentiment had scared the life out of him. Now Ian finally understood. The sound of his girls laughing in unison again after so many months of silence made him feel like he was finally beginning to shake free the demons of his past.

It was a start, anyway. All thanks to a dog and a cat.

And Rachel.

Ian's heart beat hard in the velvety night—so hard that he could hear it pounding out its *thump-thump* rhythm. Little by little, he was coming alive again. Step-by-step, day by day, breath by breath, beat by beat.

It took him a moment to realize that the *thump-thump* he was hearing wasn't actually his heartbeat. He sat up in bed, listening closely. The sound seemed to be coming from the mudroom.

Uh-oh.

He threw off the covers and shoved his feet into slippers. Pepper and Salty were supposed to be asleep in their crate, not having a party. He needed to see what exactly was going on in there.

When Ian left his bedroom and spotted a sliver of light shining beneath the closed door that led from the kitchen to the mudroom, he was sure he had the answer.

"Girls, it's late. You're supposed to be in bed. There will be plenty of time to play with Pepper and Salty in the morning," he said in his sternest dad-voice as he tied the belt around his bathrobe with a firm yank.

Then Ian swung the door open, ready to physically carry the twins back to bed if he had to. He really needed to get some sleep. They all did. He had a big work presentation coming up next week, and Annie and Abby would be cranky in the morning if they were up all night. Rachel had enough on her hands with two toddlers and two new pets in the household without adding a heaping dose of sleep deprivation among everyone in her charge.

Ian squinted against the flood of light spilling through the open doorway, and it took a beat to realize that the twins were nowhere to be seen. Instead, Rachel was crouched in front of the crate in a flowing white nightgown trimmed with lace and pale blue satin bows on the shoulders. She was petting Pepper through the bars of the crate, and the dog's tail beat against the floor in glee.

Thump-thump-thump.

Not Ian's heart, but at the sight before him, a sweet ache tugged at his chest all the same.

"Well, well." He felt his mouth curve into a sleepy grin. "What do we have here?"

"Oh. Um. Hi, there." Rachel flew to her feet. In her diaphanous white nightie, she looked more like an angel than his nanny.

His nanny.

His.

The word lodged itself in Ian's heart.

He cleared his throat. "Hi."

He should leave and let her have her private moment with the dog and cat. It was after midnight. But his feet somehow refused to budge.

"I couldn't sleep." She took a deep breath and wrapped her arms around herself.

Ian couldn't stop looking at those blue satin bows.

He could practically feel the smooth fabric against his fingertips as he imagined tugging gently at them and watching the gown come undone. Falling into a whisper at her feet.

Rachel's cheeks went pink as if she could read his mind. Or maybe, just maybe, they were both imagining the same thing. "I hope I didn't disturb you. I kept thinking about Pepper and Salty and wondering if they were okay in here all alone."

"You didn't disturb me at all." He ran a hand through his hair. Did he have bed head? Morning breath? Gosh, he hoped not. "I couldn't sleep, either."

Salty pawed at the bars of the crate and let out a soft meow.

Rachel arched an eyebrow. "Looks like we're not the only ones."

Ian managed to tear his gaze away from Rachel long enough to take in the sight of the dog and cat, who both appeared to be doing their best to give him sad, puppy-dog eyes even though only one of them was, in fact, canine.

"Should we let them out?" he heard himself say.

Bad idea. Terrible. The number one rule of training a pet was consistency. That's what the flyer Bethany from Furever Paws had given him said, anyway. If he let them out now, they might never want to sleep in here again.

"Just for a few minutes, maybe?" The corners of Rachel's pretty pink mouth tugged into a grin.

"Why do I have a feeling we're going to regret this?" Ian said as he stepped closer to her and un-latched the crate.

In less than a second, the cat was winding his way through Rachel's slender legs, while Pepper's tail banged against Ian's shins as he and Rachel exchanged goofy grins. She was so close—close enough for him to reach out and cup her cheek if he dared. Run the pad of his thumb over the lush swell of her bottom lip…

I want to kiss her. The thought slammed into Ian so hard that he nearly rocked backward on his feet. He wasn't sure he'd ever wanted to kiss a woman so much in his life.

"When I was a little girl and I couldn't sleep, sometimes I'd sneak into the kitchen and make my-self a bowl of ice cream. It always worked like a charm." Rachel's gaze flitted toward the kitchen and then back at Ian. Mischief danced in the emerald depths of her irises.

She'd spoken so infrequently about her life be-fore she'd arrived in Spring Forest that this small secret felt almost like a gift. Ian's hands clenched into fists at his sides, as if he could hold on tightly to her words…to this wholly unexpected and dream-like moment.

"Ice cream is always a good idea. That's what my daughters tell me, anyway." He gave a small nod toward the freezer, loaded with Elma's casseroles and Tupperware containers full of her homemade soup. But Ian knew there had to be a carton of Rocky Road in there somewhere. God willing.

"Shall we?"

Rachel was stirring eggs at the stove the following morning when Ian walked into the kitchen dressed for work.

"Good morning," she said and tried her best not to think about the fact that her lips still tasted like marshmallows and chocolate from their late-night ice cream date. Decadent, delicious and oh-so-sweet.

It was not *a date*, she reminded herself. *More like a happy accident.*

The entire episode had been completely innocent. They'd each eaten a towering amount of Rocky Road and shared stories from their respective childhoods while Pepper and Salty snuggled next to their feet underneath the table.

Every so often Pepper nudged Rachel's foot with her head, angling for a pat. They left the lights in the kitchen off and kept their voices low, so as not to wake the children. And there'd just been something so nice and intimate about exchanging whispers while moonlight streamed in from the skylight.

After they parted and Rachel had returned to the carriage house, she'd slept more soundly than she had in as long as she could remember.

You're safe here, she reminded herself. *That's why you feel so at peace.*

But deep down, Rachel knew there was more to her feelings than simple security. More than gratitude. Just…more.

"Good morning." Ian sent her a secret smile and then greeted Annie and Abby with kisses to the tops of their heads.

Pepper's tail beat happily against the floor, but she didn't budge from her spot beside Annie's chair. Similarly, Salty stayed put beneath Abby's seat, with his dark tail curled protectively around the leg of her chair.

"You missed your run this morning," Rachel said as she divided the scrambled eggs into equal-sized servings on the twins' *Angelina Ballerina* plates.

"Yeah." Ian straightened the knot in his tie and began sliding his arms into his suit jacket. "For some reason, I couldn't quite get out of bed when my alarm went off."

A warm, fuzzy feeling came over Rachel. So she hadn't dreamed that midnight ice cream encounter, after all. It had been real.

All of this was real.

Maybe she wouldn't have to leave Spring Forest

as soon as she'd planned. A girl could dream, right? "Funny, I had the exact same problem."

"Did you, now?" Ian's eyes met hers, and there it was again—that flood of warmth that made her feel like a cat resting languidly in the sunshine.

Rachel blinked and tried to shake it off. She was at work. This was her *job*, not the set of an idealized family sitcom.

"Can I make you some eggs?" She gestured toward the stove with the spatula in her hand.

"Thank you, but no. I need to get to the office." Ian glanced at the fancy silver watch he always wore but made no move to head toward the back door. "What's on the agenda for you and the girls today? Anything special?"

"We were just talking about that before you walked in." Rachel aimed her gaze at Annie and Abby. Abby pushed her eggs around her plate with her spoon, while Annie held a bite of her toast between her thumb and forefinger. Rachel had a sneaking suspicion the toddler had been planning on sneaking the morsel to Pepper, but as soon as Rachel arched a brow, Annie popped it into her own mouth instead. "Weren't we, girls?"

"Yes, Daddy." Abby kicked her legs back and forth under her chair.

Annie nodded quietly.

Rachel glanced back at Ian. "We've decided we're going to try and bathe Pepper today."

Pepper cocked her head at the sound of her name. Ian tilted his in near unison, and Rachel couldn't help but laugh.

"Are you joking?" Ian asked.

"Nope. I hate to tell you this, but after the events of last night, your new dog smells an awful lot like chicken tetrazzini." Rachel shrugged. "It's kind of necessary."

"I love chicken pasketti," Abby said.

"Me too," Annie said in a timid little voice. A victory, all the same.

"Yes, you do." Ian offered Annie a broad smile. "And apparently, so do Pepper and Salty."

Both girls snickered into their tiny hands, no doubt remembering the more comical parts of Elma's surprise dinner visit.

Rachel felt for the poor woman. She always seemed to turn up at the worst possible moments. It was a wonder she hadn't barged in at midnight and found Rachel and Ian eating ice cream in their pajamas. Wouldn't that have been lovely?

We weren't doing anything wrong, Rachel reminded herself. Still, the very thought of Elma finding them together like that left her with a knot in the pit of her stomach.

"I'm not letting you bathe Pepper all by yourself." Ian shook his head. "No way. I ask enough of you as it is. Dog bathing is above and beyond the call of duty."

"Oh, you'd like us to hold off until you get home from work so you can join us?" Rachel teased. "Done."

"Not that, either." Ian laughed. For a man operating on such little sleep, he seemed to be in an awfully good mood. He was almost unrecognizable as the same harried father who'd plowed into Rachel just a few short weeks ago. "There's a place in town called Barkyard Boarding. They do pet boarding, grooming and maybe even some training, I think? I'm not sure, but I know for a fact they can give Pepper a bath."

"That sounds great. Maybe the girls could see a few more animals," Rachel said.

"Yay!" Abby held up her pink toddler fork in triumph.

"How about it, Annie? Do you want to take Pepper to Barkyard Boarding today?" Ian glanced from Annie to Pepper and back again, waiting patiently for his daughter to answer.

It took a lot less than six seconds before Annie nodded. "Yes, please."

"Rub a dub dub, a puppy in a tub," Abby began singing, but instead of belting it out like she normally did when she sang, it was more of a whisper instead of a shout. Salty immediately started purring.

Ian and Rachel exchanged another meaningful look.

"Thank you," he murmured.

And Rachel wanted to tell him that the girls' behavior wasn't changing because of anything she'd done. All they'd needed was a little time and patience. A dog and a cat. And a father who'd finally begun to heal…just a little bit.

Ian's little family wasn't perfect. Not by a long shot. Annie still spoke very little. But she made more eye contact with the people around her every day, and it was already clear that Pepper had given her a major boost in confidence. Salty had an uncanny calming effect on Abby. And Ian?

Rachel was beginning to see him for the person he really was—a man who left her breathless.

The Parsons were going to be just fine. Rachel only wished she could say the same for herself.

Chapter Ten

Barkyard Boarding was located in downtown Spring Forest, just off Main Street on a shady boulevard called Windsor Terrace. Massive trees lined the street on either side, with limbs dripping Spanish moss. It made Rachel want to sit in a rocking chair on one of the older house's wide front porches and drink a frosty glass of sweet tea.

Considering she was currently in charge of two small children and a somewhat-reluctant rescue dog, that wasn't going to happen.

"Come on, Pepper. You can do it. Everything is going to be just fine." Rachel bent to scratch the sweet black Lab between the ears.

The pup's big brown eyes cut toward the long tan building with a metal roof where she had an appointment to be bathed in just under ten minutes. Then she looked back up at Rachel with such a pitiful expression that Rachel nearly relented and let her trot back to the car. Chicken tetrazzini wasn't such a terrible aroma, was it?

The poor dog seemed lost without her feline companion. No wonder they hadn't wanted to separate the adorable duo at Furever Paws.

"Pep-per," Abby groaned and then sighed dramatically when the dog still refused to budge from the middle of the sidewalk.

"Let's be patient, Abby. Pepper is just a little bit nervous." Rachel ran a comforting hand over the soft fur on the dog's head. "This is sort of like the first day of school for her. Do you remember how you felt on your first day of preschool?"

In Rachel's experience, even boisterous kids like Abby had at least a little trouble adjusting to a new school environment. Socialization and confidence building were two of the most important goals of the entire preschool experience. A little reticence in the beginning was to be expected. Most children— Annie being the exception, of course—quickly blossomed.

Abby's little forehead scrunched, and Rachel could practically see the wheels turning in her head.

Someday she'd be ready to return to a classroom preschool setting. Rachel firmly believed that. But for now, at least, Annie seemed to remember feeling every bit as hesitant as Pepper clearly did right now.

Annie stepped closer to the big dog, lifted one of her floppy ears and whispered directly into Pepper's ear canal, "Pepper get bath. Good Pepper."

The dog turned and swiped Annie's face with a lick of her big pink tongue. Then Annie took a step toward the Barkyard's door and Pepper followed. Fifteen or so baby steps later, they were all inside.

Ian would have loved to see this.

Rachel's throat went thick. Then she shook off the thought, because the tall man at the front desk was looking at her, expecting her to say something instead of standing there all dreamy-eyed over her boss and a lovely little family she wasn't an actual part of.

"Hi, I'm Shane. Welcome to Barkyard Boarding." He waved his hands, encompassing the bright reception area. To the right of the lobby, dogs stood on tables getting their coats trimmed in a row of grooming rooms. The boarding area spread out to the left. Through the lobby's floor-to-ceiling windows, Rachel spotted a small group of dogs romping off-leash in a play area while several employees wearing Barkyard Boarding T-shirts supervised the interaction.

"Yes, hello. I'm Rachel, the nanny for the Parsons family. I called earlier and made an appointment for a bath."

"Ah, yes. This must be Pepper." The man came around from behind the desk and bent down to the dog's level.

"She's shy," Abby said.

"I see that." The man winked. "That's okay. Some of my favorite dogs are shy. Some of my favorite people are too."

The corners of Annie's mouth inched into a smile.

"We just adopted Pepper from Furever Paws yesterday, along with a cat named Salty." Rachel swallowed. Had she just said *we*? Again? She really needed to stop thinking that way. "I mean, the family adopted her."

"I remember her from the big rescue in Wendell a few months ago. The sheriff's department shut down a huge breeding operation. The conditions were awful." Shane gave Rachel a meaningful glance. Clearly, he could have elaborated but probably thought it best not to since the children were present. "I'm glad Pepper and Salty found a good home."

"They couldn't ask for a better family," Rachel said.

"Can I offer Pepper a treat?" Shane reached into the pocket of his jeans.

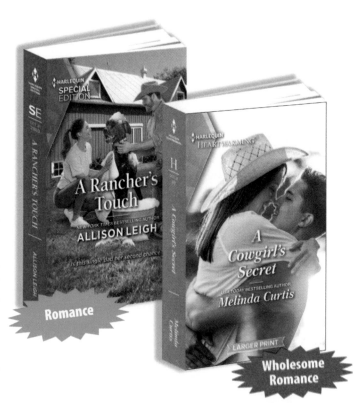

Get ready to relax and indulge with your FREE BOOKS and more!

Claim up to FOUR NEW BOOKS & TWO MYSTERY GIFTS – absolutely FREE!

Dear Reader,

We both know life can be difficult at times. That's why it's important to treat yourself so you can relax and recharge once in a while.

And I'd like to help you do this by sending you this amazing offer of up to FOUR brand new full length FREE BOOKS that WE pay for.

This is everything I have ready to send to you right now:

Try **Harlequin® Special Edition** books featuring comfort and strength in the support of loved ones and enjoying the journey no matter what life throws your way.

Try **Harlequin® Heartwarming™ Larger-Print** books featuring uplifting stories where the bonds of friendship, family and community unite.

Or TRY BOTH!

All we ask in return is that you answer 4 simple questions on the attached Treat Yourself survey. You'll get **Two Free Books** and **Two Mystery Gifts** from each series you try, *altogether worth over $20!* Who could pass up a deal like that?

Sincerely,

Pam Powers

Harlequin Reader Service

Treat Yourself to Free Books and Free Gifts.

Answer 4 fun questions and get rewarded.

	YES	NO
1. I LOVE reading a good book.	○	○
2. I indulge and "treat" myself often.	○	○
3. I love getting FREE things.	○	○
4. Reading is one of my favorite activities.	○	○

TREAT YOURSELF • Pick your 2 Free Books...

Yes! Please send me my Free Books from each series I select and Free Mystery Gifts. I understand that I am under no obligation to buy anything, as explained on the back of this card.

Which do you prefer?

❏ **Harlequin® Special Edition** 235/335 HDL GRCC
❏ **Harlequin® Heartwarming™ Larger-Print** 161/361 HDL GRCC
❏ **Try Both** 235/335 & 161/361 HDL GRCN

FIRST NAME   LAST NAME

ADDRESS

APT.#   CITY

STATE/PROV.   ZIP/POSTAL CODE

EMAIL ❏ Please check this box if you would like to receive newsletters and promotional emails from Harlequin Enterprises ULC and its affiliates. You can unsubscribe anytime.

"Sure. I think she'd like that." Rachel smiled at Annie and Abby. "Right, girls?"

"Pepper loves food." Abby's head bobbed up and down. "That's why she smells like pasketti."

Shane laughed and, with an open hand, he offered Pepper a bone-shaped biscuit. "Here you go, Pepper. It's not spaghetti, but it's the best I've got."

The Lab's tail waved back and forth as she tiptoed closer and took the treat. Annie grinned at her loud crunching noises while she ate.

Shane stood and rested his hands on his hips. "We'll get Pepper all cleaned up. I promise she'll have a good time. Do you have any questions for me before we walk her back to the grooming area?"

"Ian mentioned that you have training classes," Rachel said.

"Absolutely. We have weekly group classes that cover the basic commands, like sit, where we also train the dogs on walking on a loose leash. And I offer private lessons, as well." Shane regarded Pepper and shrugged one shoulder. "That might be the way to go at first, so Pepper can gain a little more confidence before you put her in a group setting."

Shane was speaking Rachel's language. This was perfect. "Could Annie participate in the training? They're really close already, and I think it would be good for both of them."

"You don't say?" Shane glanced at Annie, who'd

just wrapped her arms around Pepper's neck to give her an effusive send-off for her bath. "That's a great idea. I'd be happy to work with them. Let me check our training schedule and we'll get it on the calendar."

He strode back behind the counter, picked up an iPad and began tapping at the screen. While he scrolled through the calendar app, Rachel glanced at the various pamphlets and announcements pinned to the bulletin board behind the front desk.

One of them, in particular, caught her eye. "Doggy Fashion Show? That sounds fun."

Shane nodded without looking up from his tablet. "Yeah, it's scheduled as part of the Spring Forest Fall Festival. Regina Mackenzie is putting it together— she's a local philanthropist and handles a lot of fundraisers. This one is to raise money for Furever Paws. The dog models are all rescue pups from there, and I think they're going to have a few dog models available for adoption, as well."

Rachel's hand fluttered to her heart. "That sounds precious."

But it was taking place during the fall festival. It was late summer now. Would she even still be living in Spring Forest by then?

Not if she stuck to her plan.

Rescue dogs in costumes sounded beyond adorable, though. The twins would love it. Maybe she could nudge her departure date out just a little further.

"I'm sure it will be a big hit, *if* it actually happens." Shane sighed. "It seems Regina has left town suddenly and no one knows where she's gone. *Or* the money she's collected for the event's expenses, either."

"Oh, no." Rachel's stomach fluttered. Sudden disappearances were never a good thing. She should know. "I hope everything is okay."

Shane started to say something, but just as he was about to speak, he glanced out the window and his brow furrowed. "Actually, that's Regina's niece—and also her assistant, I guess, though I'm not sure if that's her official title—who's about to walk through the front door."

Rachel turned to see a petite young woman with waves of thick, dark hair entering the lobby. Her brown eyes lit up the second she spotted Pepper. "Oh, look at you! What a cutie."

Pepper's tail wagged.

"Hi, Elise." Shane held up a hand. "This is Rachel, Annie and Abby. Pepper here is about to get a bath."

Just then, one of Shane's employees came to escort Pepper to the grooming area. Rachel handed over the leash and kept an eye on the twins as they flanked Pepper on either side all the way to her bath.

"What a sweet dog," Elise said. "And your daughters are so good with her."

"Oh, I'm just the nanny," Rachel said, wishing there was a way to make the distinction without sounding like the girls weren't an important part of her life. Then again, maybe she needed a periodic reminder of what her role truly was. "But yes, they're great with animals. Are you here to pick up your dog?"

"No, actually." Elise smiled shyly and a little awkwardly in Shane's direction, looking like a little sister who'd come to ask her brother for a favor. "I'm hoping Barkyard Boarding might be looking for some front desk help. I really need a job since my aunt…well, you know."

"Oh." Shane glanced down at the piles of paper and dog leashes stacked on the reception desk. "Actually, we might. Let me finish with Rachel here, and then we'll chat."

Elise looked relieved and stepped back to let Shane and Rachel finish. "I've got an opening Saturday at ten in the morning for a thirty-minute training session if that works for you?" Shane said.

"Perfect." At that moment, Annie and Abby skipped back to the front desk from the grooming area, hand in hand. But their little-girl giggles turned into cries of surprise and alarm when a tiny dachshund, clearly halfway through his bath and wanting not a moment more of it, came barreling down the hall, tangling himself up in the twins' feet as he dashed toward freedom.

Abby lost her balance and landed right on her backside, where she immediately started crying. Annie, clearly worried over her twin, looked on the verge of tears herself. Rachel rushed over to them and started slipping herself in the suds the little wiener dog was still shedding. Flinging her arms out to catch her balance, she smacked right into Shane, who was barely able to keep them both upright.

The only one who kept her head was Elise, who scooped up the dog with remarkable ease. The squirming animal settled down right away when Elise rubbed him behind his ears.

"You're a lifesaver," a frantic-looking woman said as she came over to take the dog. This, Rachel realized, must be the groomer who had let the dog slip away from her in the first place. With her arms full of dachshund, she turned to Shane, her face flushed fire-engine red. "Mr. Dupree, I'm so, so sorry. I don't know how he got away from me. I swear, I had him, but then he—"

Shane chuckled. "It's okay, Charlene. It happens to the best of us. You're not in trouble." Then he turned to Elise. "As for you...you're hired."

As Rachel watched, Elise's face lit up in a wide smile, and even though they'd just met, Rachel returned it. She knew what it was like to be desperate for work. The more she thought about leaving Spring Forest, the more she dreaded starting over again.

The thought of it kept running through her head as she comforted Abby and got her and Annie back on their feet. A new job. A new town. Maybe even a new name.

She'd done it once, and she could do it again. It had to get easier, didn't it? With enough practice, even the hardest things eventually became second nature.

But no matter how many times she uprooted herself, no matter how many new children she cared for, no matter how many new towns she learned to navigate on her vintage beach cruiser bicycle, none of them would feel quite like this special place…

Like home.

"You should have seen Annie today. Pepper was afraid to go inside the building when we went to Barkyard Boarding, and she guided the poor dog inside, with tiny baby steps." Rachel drizzled chocolate syrup over her bowl of ice cream and then slid the bottle across the table toward Ian. "Pepper is definitely helping her come out of her shell."

"You realize it's not just Pepper, don't you? The girls adore you. You're wonderful with Annie—with *both* the twins," Ian said.

His fingertips brushed against hers as he took hold of the chocolate syrup. Was she just imagining things, or did they both seem to linger a little longer than necessary, reluctant to pull their hands away?

Chocolate dripped down the neck of the bottle. When it drizzled onto their fingers, they finally broke contact.

"Oops." Rachel licked the syrup from her fingertip.

Ian didn't move a muscle as his gaze zeroed in on her mouth, her tongue. His eyes went molten, and then in a flash, he cleared his throat and commenced with upending the syrup bottle and dousing his bowl of ice cream with a flood of chocolate.

Pepper scrambled to her feet and poked her nose over the edge of the table, clearly interested in what they were eating.

"Sorry, girl." Rachel ran a hand over the dog's soft black fur. "Chocolate is bad for dogs."

Salty let loose with a sonorous meow.

Ian pointed his spoon at him. "Cats, too, I'm afraid."

Rachel cocked her head, and Pepper mirrored the movement with perfect canine precision. "Is that true? I knew dogs couldn't eat chocolate, but I'm not as up on my feline facts as I probably should be."

"Yup." Ian nodded. "Chocolate contains a chemical called theobromine. It's poisonous to both dogs and cats when consumed in large quantities."

Rachel narrowed her gaze at him. "Why did that just come out like you'd read it straight from a book?"

Ian's grin turned sheepish. "Maybe because I've been doing a little late-night reading on pet care?"

Adorable.

"You mean when you're not sneaking into the kitchen to check on the dog and cat in the middle of the night?" Rachel cast a meaningful glance at their twin bowls of ice cream.

"I was afraid if I didn't stay up reading after the girls went to bed, I might fall asleep and miss this." He swirled his spoon to encompass the entire cozy scene.

Rachel went warm and fuzzy all over. What were they *doing*? Salty and Pepper were adjusting to their new home just fine. They didn't need any human help with that. Yet here she and Ian were, pretending to check on the animals so they could share late-night ice cream together. All alone. No kids, no Elma. Their only chaperones were the dog and cat.

Rachel had never worked as a nanny before now, but she was fairly certain this wasn't ordinarily part of the job description. She couldn't bring herself to care, though. These late-night ice cream dates were becoming the highlight of her day—even more so, now that she knew Ian was determined not to fall asleep and miss them.

"What else have you learned about pet care?" she asked, smiling into her mint chocolate chip.

"Loads," Ian said.

"Such as?"

"Practical things, like how to train a dog to settle politely when the family is sharing a meal."

They swiveled their heads in unison toward Pepper, who'd commenced with resting her chin on the edge of the table. The Labrador's warm brown eyes darted from Ian to Rachel and back again, and she let out a sigh.

"Nailing that one, I see." Rachel laughed.

Ian held up his hands. "I said I'd learned how. I never pretended to have actually put it into practice."

Something told Rachel that the only way to get Pepper to "settle politely" while the family was sitting at the table was to make sure she was tucked as closely to Annie as possible. The dog would Velcro herself to the little girl if she could.

"Speaking of training, Shane at Barkyard Boarding told me that he does private obedience lessons. I thought it might be a good idea to schedule a few for Pepper and Annie," Rachel said.

Ian looked at the dog. "Do you want to go to school, Pepper?"

Pepper lifted her chin from the table and tilted her head at the sound of his voice saying her name.

"I think she's into it. Poor thing doesn't realize that the Parsons haven't had such a great track record with school lately," Ian said.

That's right. The girls and their problems in the classroom were the entire reason that Rachel was sitting here, sharing midnight ice cream sundaes with their father. Somehow, that kept slipping her mind. This was starting to feel less like a job every day and more like she belonged in the big house in Kingdom Creek with Ian and his family.

Remember who you are and where you came from. This isn't forever. It can't be.

"The lessons will be fun," Rachel said. If Ian noticed the suddenly forced enthusiasm in her voice, his expression didn't show it. He just kept looking at her with the same warmth in his eyes while his ice cream melted in its bowl. "Helping train Pepper will be good for Annie. It will be a great chance for her to work on her speaking voice and stringing words together into sentences. She loves Pepper, so I know she'll really make the effort to help her."

Ian nodded. "I'm impressed. I never would have thought of that. It sounds like a great idea."

"Good, because the lessons start this weekend. The only day Shane had available was Saturday. I hope that's okay."

"Of course it's okay. I'm glad I'll get to be there." Ian took another bite of his sundae. Both of their bowls were nearly empty.

Rachel found herself taking smaller and smaller bites, wanting to draw out their conversation as long as possible. "So tell me more about Bunny and Stew. At Furever Paws, Bunny seemed to say they were just friends, but I sensed a definite spark there."

"Everyone does." Ian nodded. "Bunny and Stew went away together on a big RV trip across the country a few months ago. It was a big romantic thing— they'd been emailing for months and they finally got together. But when she came back, she was alone. Stew came chasing after her not much later. She calls him her 'special someone,' but he's also kind of a mystery man. I told you she'd never met an animal— or in this case, a person—she didn't want to rescue."

"He seems to adore her." Rachel smiled to herself. She liked the idea of someone finding love late in life. It made her hopeful for her own future. Falling for someone anytime soon wasn't a possibility, with good reason. But maybe someday…someway…

She pushed her bowl away, suddenly not feeling very hungry anymore.

"According to Elma, Stew is head over heels for Bunny. He's made it clear that he's ready to stop traveling and settle down as long as Bunny is by his side." Ian stood to carry their dishes to the sink.

"Bunny is a little hesitant. I think living together in an RV for so long was a bit of a challenge."

"How does Elma know all of this?" Rachel grabbed a dish towel as Ian started rinsing their bowls. He handed her a spoon and she dried it, as if they'd stood at the sink together like this a million times before.

Ian snorted. "Have you met my mother-in-law? Nothing happens in Spring Forest without Elma Miller knowing about it."

Nothing?

The bowl in Rachel's hand slipped out of her grasp, and Ian managed to catch it before it crashed to the floor.

"Sorry. I don't know why I'm so clumsy all of a sudden." Rachel's face went warm.

Ian waved a hand and went back to washing the dishes. "It's nothing. Don't worry about it."

But there was a lot to worry about, especially if Elma truly did have a knack for finding out secret information. She certainly had the motivation to go digging into Rachel's past—and to keep digging until she found some dirt. Rachel really should have realized this could be a potential problem before now. Elma obviously liked poking her nose into things.

You're letting your guard down, and you should know better.

"Hey, are you okay? You looked lost for a second there." Ian touched her chin with the tip of his finger, dragging her gaze toward his.

A sudsy soap bubble drifted toward the ceiling, as fragile and breakable as the attraction that seemed to be building between them. Then the bubble popped, and Rachel took a backward step.

"Fine. Just tired, I guess." She faked a yawn.

"I suppose that makes sense, since it's one in the morning." Ian dipped his head to search her gaze. "See you tomorrow night? Same place, same time?"

He was asking her to drop the pretense that they were doing this for the pets. If she said yes, they were going to agree to meet, just like a real date.

But he was giving her a choice, because he was a gentleman. She was his employee, and he didn't want to push her into anything she didn't want. Rachel could always say no. If she did, then she knew without a doubt that everything would go back to the way it was before. She'd be his nanny and nothing else.

That wasn't what she wanted, though.

"Yes," she murmured, resting a palm against Ian's broad chest. Then she stepped closer, rose up on tiptoe and brushed her lips against his cheek. "Good night."

Just one more night, she told herself. *Just one more bowl of ice cream.*

And as she walked back to the carriage house under a blue Carolina moon, she even pretended to believe it.

Chapter Eleven

Ian was dating his nanny.

It felt that way, anyway. Ian hadn't actually dated in years, so he couldn't be sure. But the rush of pleasure he felt every time Rachel was near seemed vaguely familiar, as did his anticipation of their secret late-night meetings.

Ice cream in the middle of the night was hardly a proper date, though. Ian longed to ask her out to dinner. He wanted to treat her to a real evening out. A candlelight dinner at Veniero's, perhaps. She deserved a fancy meal. She deserved everything.

He didn't dare suggest it. Every time it felt like

he and Rachel were growing closer, she seemed to withdraw ever so slightly. It felt like they were taking two steps forward and one step back. Was romance always like this? Ian couldn't be sure. He'd been just a boy the last time he'd fallen in love. Now he was a grown man, and he still didn't seem to have the first clue what he was doing.

Love? Really?

He wasn't in love. He couldn't be. After Serena had died, he'd sworn never to make that mistake again. Having his life upended once was enough, thank you very much. What little emotional energy he had left needed to go to his daughters.

He couldn't seem to stop himself when it came to Rachel, though. There was just something about her that made him feel new again. Hopeful, even after everything he'd been through. It scared him as much as it enthralled him. He felt like he was going off the rails, and all he'd done was share a few innocent bowls of ice cream.

Still, there was an undeniable spring in his step as he made breakfast for Annie and Abby on Saturday morning. Saturday was one of Rachel's days off, and usually, the twins had cereal or one of Elma's famous hash brown casseroles, since there always seemed to be one of those tucked into Ian's fridge somewhere. But Ian felt like tackling something more adventurous this morning.

Something special.

"Kitty!" Abby cried when he slid her plate in front of her. "A pancake kitty!"

"It sure is." Ian grinned down at his slightly messy masterpiece.

One big pancake served as the kitten's face, and he'd cut a smaller pancake into twin triangles for the cat's ears. Two blueberries for eyes and a strawberry sliced into a triangle for the nose, and voilà. He'd created a pancake version of Salty.

"And for you, my dear Annie—a pancake puppy." Ian set the plate in his other hand down on the table in front of Annie.

Her eyes went wide.

"Pepper!" She pointed at the dog he'd fashioned from a large pancake as a face, topped by a smaller one to represent the pup's muzzle. Instead of triangle ears like the cat, Ian had cut a round pancake in half to make two floppy Labrador ears. A plump strawberry half represented the dog's dangling pink tongue.

Pepper looked at the pancake and appeared to aim some serious side-eye at Ian.

"It's your spitting image," Ian said, pointing at the dog with his spatula.

The animals had lived under his roof for less than a week and already Ian was talking to them on a regular basis. Oh, how things had changed around here.

"I don't want to eat Salty, Daddy. He's too pretty," Abby said, gingerly poking at her pancake with her fork.

"Don't worry. We'll have them again sometime." Ian glanced at the time on his phone. "Pepper's obedience training is in a little more than an hour. We all need to be big and strong for that, so you need to eat your breakfast. Okay, girls?"

"Okay, Daddy." Abby stabbed her fork into her kitten's strawberry nose, just as Salty let out a timely meow.

Annie giggled. She poised her own fork above her doggy pancake, but before she could dig in, there was a quiet tap on the back door.

Ian's heart leaped in his chest. It had to be Rachel. The only other person who ever came to his back door was Elma, and in true Elma fashion, she never bothered to knock.

"Come in," he said and turned another pancake from the skillet onto a plate. As long as she was here instead of the carriage house, he may as well offer her some breakfast. He quickly set to work on decorating the pancake.

Rachel opened the door just enough to poke her head inside. "Sorry to interrupt. I think I left the book I'm reading in the girls' playroom and—"

"Miss Rachel, Daddy made breakfast. See?" Abby pointed at her plate.

"Sweetheart, try not to interrupt Miss Rachel when she's speaking. Remember?" Ian cast a pointed glance at Abby and then turned to offer Rachel a plate. "Would you care to join us?"

Rachel's gaze darted to the plate and she laughed. "Is that a *lion*?"

He glanced down at the big round pancake face, surrounded by a spiky circle of mane fashioned from sliced strawberries. His best attempt yet.

"Indeed it is." He took another plate from the counter and offered it up for her inspection. "Unless you prefer an inchworm?"

Rachel took in the caterpillar he'd made from half a dozen overlapping silver-dollar pancakes with tiny feet made of raisins and shook her head. "There's no way I can turn this down. Are you sure you don't mind? I don't want to interrupt family time."

You are *family.* Ian nearly said it, but he didn't want to be presumptuous—not when Rachel sometimes seemed like a skittish animal herself.

So instead, he shrugged and said, "There's no way we can eat this entire zoo ourselves. Come on in."

Minutes later, they were all seated at the table, eating breakfast together as if it was any ordinary weekend and Ian and Rachel were any ordinary couple. Ian reminded himself that they weren't. Spending so much time with her when she was off the clock was messing with his head, that's all.

But sitting beside her felt so natural. So right. As the meal drew to a close, he wasn't ready for her to go. They had Pepper's class, though. He needed to get the girls loaded up in their car seats and coax Pepper into the back seat between them.

"Girls, why don't you go wash up while I get Pepper's treats packed for her lesson?" Ian said as he stood to clear the table.

Rachel jumped to her feet. "Here, let me help. I almost forgot about Pepper's class. You all need to get going soon, right?"

Ian shook his head. "It's your day off. You don't have to take care of us during your free time."

"I want to, though," Rachel said, and her cheeks immediately went pink. "I mean, it's no trouble at all. Plus, you cooked. It's only fair that I clean up the mess. I want you all to have a great time at dog class."

"Miss Rachel come with us." Abby's little mouth tipped into a frown.

Annie's big blue eyes glittered with alarm. Even Pepper seemed to gaze up at her with big, puppy-dog eyes.

"It's Rachel's day off, girls," Ian said. As much as he wanted to spend time with her, he didn't want his entire household to guilt her into it.

Rachel stood beside him, her eyes still as wide as a deer in headlights.

She managed to smile at Annie and Abby. "I don't want to intrude on your alone time with your dad."

Abby sighed mightily. Then Annie slid down from her chair, walked toward Rachel and took her by the hand.

"Please come with us, Miss Rachel," she said in a tiny, barely audible voice.

But it was a full sentence—not just a word or a phrase. Sentences were still coming few and far between for Annie, and the fact that she'd felt confident enough to voice her desire for Rachel to attend obedience class with them made Ian's chest feel full to the brim.

He glanced at Rachel. "I don't want you to feel obligated, but if you're free, we'd love for you to come along."

"Are you kidding?" Rachel bent down so she was eye level with Annie. "I'd love to come watch you train Pepper. Thank you so much for inviting me."

Annie beamed and hugged Rachel's neck. Rachel's eyes squeezed closed as she embraced his little girl, and Ian knew he should thank her. He tried his best, but he couldn't seem to find the words.

So instead, when she opened her eyes, he blew her a kiss. It was the smallest of movements—just a quick pucker of his lips. But the sparkle in Rachel's eyes told him it had landed right on target.

Squarely in her heart.

Pepper seemed less dubious about going inside Barkyard Boarding than she had the first time, but Annie stayed right by the dog's side with her tiny hand planted on Pepper's back as they walked into the building.

While Ian had gotten the girls ready to attend class, Rachel had cut hot dogs and string cheese into small, bite-size pieces for training treats, which were now tucked into her handbag. When they entered the building, Shane was at the front desk deep in conversation with Elise about the upcoming Doggy Fashion Show. Once he looked up and ushered them into the training area, Rachel handed him the baggie of treats.

"Annie might need a little help giving those to Pepper at the proper time," Rachel said.

Ian shot Shane a meaningful look. "If it were up to her, she would probably let Pepper stick her entire snout into that baggie and eat them all in one go."

Shane laughed. "Understood." He squatted to look Annie directly in the eye. "Are you ready to teach Pepper a few new tricks today, Annie?"

Annie nodded.

"Okay, then. Ian, Rachel and Abby, why don't

you take a seat at the back of the room?" Shane motioned toward a row of chairs behind them. "Annie and I can take it from here."

Ian and Rachel exchanged a glance. She could tell he wasn't convinced that Annie would be able to train the dog without help from either of them, but Rachel knew they needed to give her a chance.

"Super. We'll be right here, watching. You'll do great, Annie." Rachel ruffled Annie's soft blond hair. "You and Pepper make an awesome team."

Pepper panted happily at the sound of her name, but she remained glued to Annie's side as Rachel, Ian and Abby got settled in their chairs a few yards away.

"The first thing we're going to teach Pepper is how to respond to her name," Shane said.

Annie nodded, her petite brow furrowed in concentration.

"You're going to say her name, loud and clear, and the second she looks at you, tell her she's a good girl and give her a treat. Like this." Shane swiveled his gaze toward the dog. "Pepper?"

The Lab reluctantly dragged her attention away from Annie and looked at Shane.

"Good girl," Shane gushed and offered Pepper a bit of the string cheese from the baggie.

Pepper wagged her tail and gulped it down in a single bite, prompting a quiet laugh from Annie.

"At least she's having a good time," Ian whispered.

Rachel glanced at him. "You look like a nervous wreck. This is supposed to be fun, remember?"

"You don't think it's too much? I don't want Annie to feel pressured. I'd hate for her to lose all the great progress she's made lately." A muscle ticked in Ian's jaw. "What do you think?"

"I think it's a good thing I came along." Rachel took his hand and squeezed it. "She's doing amazing. Give her a chance. If she starts to get overwhelmed, you can jump in and help her. Part of helping Annie overcome her shyness is giving her the space to speak for herself. It requires a lot of patience."

Ian considered her words. "Not exactly my strong suit, in case you haven't noticed."

But that wasn't exactly true. In the beginning, sure, she'd thought of him as harshly impatient. But the man who'd plowed into her and sent building blocks flying everywhere wasn't the same man who'd taken the time to make animal pancakes this morning or who'd been spending his free time reading pet-training manuals and enjoying late-night ice cream sundaes.

She gave him a shoulder bump. "You don't give yourself enough credit, you know that?"

He frowned. "What do you mean?"

"I mean you're a wonderful dad, Ian. The girls are blessed to have you as their father," she said and meant every word.

He was doing exactly as she'd told him in the beginning. He'd opened himself up—to the world outside his big house in Kingdom Creek. To change. To *joy*.

And in turn, he'd shown his daughters they could do the same.

"I could kiss you right now," he whispered, and the low timbre of his voice and the way his gaze dropped to her mouth told her he was dead serious.

Heaven help her, she wanted him to. They were at a dog training class for a shelter pup and a toddler, which had to be one of the least romantic settings in the entire world. But Rachel felt like she was being swept right off her feet.

No. She took a deep breath and forced herself to look away and focus on Annie and Pepper instead of Ian's heated gaze. *You can't fall for him.*

But it was too late, wasn't it? Ian didn't need to say her name and reward her when she responded by looking his way. She was aware of him at all times. Every glance, every whisper, every touch. He was gradually becoming her compass, her true north.

She'd already fallen.

This is bad. Rachel's stomach churned. What was she going to do?

"Pepper," Annie said, loud and clear enough to be heard all the way in the back of the training room.

Pepper immediately gazed up at Annie, her own true north.

"Good girl." Annie's voice was quieter this time, but still discernible from where they sat. Shane slipped a treat into her hand and she promptly gave it to Pepper.

"Good girl, Annie!" Abby raised her fists in the air, shaking them like pom-poms.

Rachel hadn't realized she was still holding Ian's hand until she went to pull it away and join in the cheering by clapping her hands. But Ian's fingers wove even more tightly though hers, hanging on as if he were afraid to let go…

Lest she run away.

Rachel's throat grew tight, and she kept her attention on Annie and Pepper, but she squeezed his hand back as hard as she could.

I'm not going anywhere, the gesture seemed to say. She swallowed hard. *Not yet, anyway.*

Chapter Twelve

The girls and the animals kept Ian plenty busy for the remainder of the weekend. Simply making sure that Annie wasn't exhausting poor Pepper by making her practice her obedience homework from sunup to sundown was a challenge. Shane had advised that they should work on the attention exercises, plus the *sit* and *down* commands, for ten minutes a day.

The only problem seemed to be that toddlers didn't understand the concept of "ten minutes." Every time he turned around, Annie was dangling a treat in front of Pepper's nose. The Labrador was learning her commands, but at this rate, Ian was going to have to invest in some diet dog food.

Naturally, Abby decided that Pepper shouldn't be the only pet genius in the household. On Sunday morning, she began attempting to train Salty to do the tricks Pepper had mastered. When Salty proved to be of a more independent mind than Pepper, Abby decided to start awarding the cat treats for simpler tasks, like purring or kneading the sofa cushions, which, to Ian's amusement, Rachel called "making biscuits."

Training antics aside, it was a nice weekend. The best Ian had experienced in a long time, and not just because he and Rachel kept meeting for ice cream, even though she didn't work on Saturday or Sunday. When Monday morning rolled around, he felt loose, relaxed and—dare he think it?—happy.

"I think I'll invite Elma over for dinner tonight," he said as he shot Rachel a glance over the top of his coffee cup.

"Really?" Her mouth curved into a grin. "She would love that. It would be a wonderful surprise."

"Would it seriously be such a shock? I do care about her. I'm fine with having her over for dinner every now and then. The problem is that she always beats me to the punch and turns up before I have a chance to issue an invitation." Ian kept his voice low so the girls wouldn't overhear.

Not that they were paying attention. They'd spread

their alphabet building blocks onto the table and were attempting to stack them into towers.

"She knows you care, but I have a feeling she'd be delighted to get an official invitation." Rachel stirred a dollop of cream into her coffee. "Elma wants to feel like she's a part of things around here. That's all. Like she's welcomed and not just tolerated. She cares so much about this family and wants to be included. She just doesn't always go about it in the most subtle fashion."

Ian arched a brow. "So you've noticed?"

Rachel gave him a playful swat. "You're terrible."

"I'm only kidding, but I want you to know that I'm fully aware she can be—" he paused to choose his next words carefully "—*difficult* at times. And it means a lot to me that you're so patient with her."

"It's no bother. I honestly don't find her difficult at all." Rachel's gaze dropped to the contents of her coffee mug. "I suppose I can relate to how she feels."

Ian grew still. "How so?"

"Come on, Ian. Don't make me say it," she said, suddenly overly interested in refilling the water reservoir on the coffee maker.

He cupped her elbow and pulled her toward him with a gentle tug. "Talk to me. Please?"

"Fine." Her eyelashes fluttered, as if she were trying to pass her next words off as meaningless fluff.

But Ian saw past her defense mechanism. "Elma is just lonely. She wants to be part of a family."

But Rachel wasn't just talking about Elma anymore, and they both knew it.

If they'd been alone, Ian would've swept her into his arms right then and there. Even with small spectators, he was still tempted. But he didn't know if he should while the twins were there. He and Rachel hadn't discussed whatever was happening between them. Ian wasn't even altogether sure that something was, in fact, happening.

He thought so. He hoped so.

But he also knew that there was an invisible wall around Rachel that he'd yet to fully breach, and he respected her too much to put her into the potentially uncomfortable position of having his children ask why their daddy was hugging their nanny.

"Then, I'll definitely call and invite Elma over tonight for dinner. I'll pick up pizzas on the way home from work, and I'll even pretend to be contrite when she lectures me about proper toddler nutrition." Annie and Abby ate fully balanced meals on the regular, which Elma was well aware of. Pizzas were reserved for special occasions, and Ian felt like their little family was long overdue for a celebration.

"I do have one condition, though." Ian held up a finger.

Rachel regarded him through narrowed eyes. "What's the condition?"

"I want you to join us. Not as the nanny, but as a guest." He cleared his throat, nervous all of a sudden. "*My* guest."

"Elma's not ready for that," Rachel said flatly.

Ian couldn't help but wonder if, once again, she was using Elma's name in place of her own.

"I can keep a secret if you can," he said, waggling his eyebrows exaggeratedly like he was joking, when in fact, he was dead serious. "If you'd rather not share anything with Elma, we don't have to."

If Rachel wasn't ready for him to tell Elma that he had feelings for her, he'd wait. But he couldn't stand the thought of Rachel feeling lonely or excluded.

Ever.

She smiled, but it didn't reach her eyes, and it was then that Ian realized that he and Rachel had something fundamental in common. They both carried a profound sadness in their hearts. It was written in the depths of her emerald eyes. Ian could see it, because he knew the feeling well.

The difference was that Rachel knew all about his grief and the difficulties he'd faced since losing Serena, but the reasons for her sorrow were a mystery to Ian. Didn't she know that a burden shared was a burden halved? He could understand whatever had hurt her in the past. He could help her in the same way she had helped him.

If only she'd let him.

A silence stretched between them, swollen with meaning. Heavy with all the things that neither of them was ready to say. For a time, Ian had thought he'd never be able to say them again…to anyone.

But something had changed. *He'd* changed. He didn't dread waking up in the morning anymore. He wasn't bombarded with thoughts of how he was messing up his daughters' lives and failing to live up to the promises he'd made Serena. Sometimes, he even thought he might be doing a decent job at this parenting thing.

The future almost seemed like something to look forward to.

Ian set his coffee mug gently on the kitchen counter. He needed to get to the office. One of the firm's biggest clients had requested a proposal for a massive structural engineering project, and he was the lead engineer on the team. He only had a week or so to get the presentation done.

He didn't want to go, though. Not without an answer.

"What do you say?" Ian's hand twitched at his side. Rachel's lush auburn hair was piled on top of her head in a messy bun. Soft morning sunshine streamed through the window over the sink, bringing out its fiery highlights.

A wisp of a curl fell in front of her face, as shiny as a copper penny. The urge to tuck it behind her ear and let his fingertips trace the exquisite curve of her neck was so visceral that it was almost painful.

For a long moment, Rachel eyed him, and then she brushed the lock of hair from her eyes, as if she'd read his mind.

"I can keep a secret too."

I can keep a secret too.

Ian had no idea how serious Rachel had been when she'd said those words, and she hoped with all of her heart it would stay that way.

She knew it was wrong to keep things from him. He was her employer. More importantly, he was a friend—possibly more than that, if she was really being honest with herself. But she didn't know how to tell him about her past, especially now. Too much time had passed while she had stayed silent. The time for confessions had come and gone.

Not that she'd necessarily done anything that warranted confessing. After uprooting her entire life and constantly looking over her shoulder, Rachel seemed to forget that significant detail. She felt like a fugitive, but that didn't mean she actually was one. Not from the law, anyway.

Still, she hadn't exactly been truthful with Ian, and that very real fact nagged at her later that evening as she sat at the dinner table with his family.

"It was such a nice surprise getting your call today, Ian. Thank you for inviting me to dinner," Elma said as she gingerly cut a slice of pepperoni pizza with a knife and fork. "Although I don't suppose pizza is technically a meal."

Ian winked at Rachel from the head of the table. He'd called it. Elma indeed had opinions about the nutritional value of the menu, but Ian was handling the criticism with good humor, as promised.

Rachel bit back a smile. "I almost forgot. I made a nice green salad."

Elma's fork paused halfway to her mouth. "You did?"

"Yes. It's in the refrigerator. I'll just run and get it." Rachel pushed her chair back from the table and headed toward the kitchen. Pepper and Salty scrambled to their feet and followed.

She slipped Pepper a nibble of hot dog from the bag of dog treats in the fridge and then grabbed the big crystal bowl of salad from the middle shelf. When Rachel turned around to head back to the dining room, she nearly plowed straight into Ian.

"You made a salad." He glanced down at the bowl. Never had Rachel seen someone so amused by a pile of lettuce. "And you put it in a crystal serving dish."

"I figured Elma would especially appreciate the Waterford." Rachel shrugged.

"You really do understand her, don't you?" Ian took the bowl from her hands. Pepper, meanwhile, pawed at her shin, angling for another bite of hot dog. "I get the feeling you understand all of us."

A shiver coursed through Rachel. The air from the opened refrigerator door was cool on the back of her neck, yet she felt warm all over. A conversation about salad shouldn't feel this romantic.

"Maybe I do," she said.

"Do you two need any help in there?" Elma called from the dining room.

Rachel stifled a grin, and Ian coughed to cover up a laugh.

"We'll be right there. Everything is under control," he managed to call out.

Were they, though? The chills running up and down Rachel's spine told her otherwise. Nothing in her carefully ordered life seemed to be under control, and even more concerning…she was starting to think she might actually like it that way.

The rest of the meal passed in uneventful fashion, not counting Salty's ill-advised attempt to leap onto the table directly beside Elma's plate. When the plates had been cleared and the pizza boxes collapsed and deposited into the recycling bin, they gathered in the dining room again for a rousing game of Candy Land with the twins.

They hadn't played the game since Rachel's first

night with Ian and his family. It was remarkable how much Annie seemed to enjoy it, and how expressive she was in her enjoyment compared to the last time. She moved her piece around the board with a joyful *tap-tap-tap* of plastic against the game board. Her little face lit up when she reached Princess Frostine, her favorite character, all dressed up in a ball gown and tiara in the Ice Cream Sea.

She still didn't verbalize much, though. Annie saved most of her spoken words for Pepper. Rachel knew it was only a matter of time until she'd feel confident enough to express herself verbally, in complete sentences, to all the people in her life. In the meantime, the smile on her face said it all.

"Look at you, Annie. You're ahead of all of us. The Ice Cream Sea is almost the end of the game," Elma said.

"Mmm. Ice cream." Abby cast a hopeful glance in her father's direction.

"Ice cream does sound good, doesn't it?" Elma stood. "Why don't I prepare us all a little dessert? Ian, you and Rachel have done so much already tonight. I'll scoop up some ice cream. I know I've seen a carton of Rocky Road in the freezer somewhere."

Ian's eyes went comically wide, but no one seemed to notice because Annie drew a card with two red squares, the perfect combination to get her to the Candy Castle and be declared the winner.

"I win," she said in a tiny voice.

"Yes, you do," Ian said, holding his hand up for a high five.

Annie touched her palm to his with a gentle tap. Then Abby leaned over the table and gave Ian's hand a slap.

"High five, Daddy." She giggled.

"High fives all around," he said as he slapped his own hand, prompting more laughter from Abby and a quiet smile from Annie.

Elma sashayed back into the living room, juggling five bowls. "Here we go, but there was barely enough ice cream to go around. It's the strangest thing. I was sure there were at least two full cartons in the freezer the last time I looked."

Rachel focused intently on the dish of ice cream Elma placed in front of her. If she dared to look at Ian, she might lose her composure and give them both away.

"I know what happened to it," Ian said.

Rachel shoved a spoonful of Rocky Road into her mouth.

"What, Daddy?" Abby said as she scraped her spoon along the inside of her near-empty bowl.

"Pepper must have eaten it. Obviously." Ian narrowed his gaze in the dog's direction. "She's eaten pretty much everything else in this house."

Pepper stood and wagged her tail, happy to be

part of the conversation, even if it meant she'd been assigned the role of scapegoat.

"No, she didn't, Daddy." Abby kicked her legs under the table, bobbing up and down in her chair. "Daddy's silly."

"He is, isn't he?" Elma said.

"It's okay. It doesn't matter if we're low on ice cream, because it's way past time for two little girls to get ready for bed." Ian stood and gathered the empty ice cream bowls while Rachel started putting the board game away.

"So soon?" Elma said.

"It's almost nine." Ian tapped his watch. "Don't worry. We'll do this again soon."

"That would be nice." Elma nodded. "Come along, girls. I'll help you get dressed for bed."

Rachel almost didn't know what to do with herself. It felt strange letting Elma take over the twins' bedtime ritual, since more often than not, Rachel stayed a bit late to help get the girls settled for the night. But she reminded herself she was a guest this evening, not an employee. Even so, she helped Ian get the dessert dishes cleaned up. He washed while she dried, just like they did after their midnight ice cream dates. It was starting to feel like a sacred ritual, their own secret routine.

Abby, Annie, Salty and Pepper bounded into the kitchen right as they were finishing up. Elma trailed not far behind.

"It looks like everyone is ready for bed." Ian scooped Abby into his arms and kissed one of her plump cheeks.

"Good night, Daddy," she said in her singsong voice.

"Night night, pumpkin," Ian said.

And as he was setting her gently back down on the floor, another little voice rang out in the sparkling kitchen.

"Daddy, Pepper sleep with me tonight?"

Every head in the room turned toward Annie.

She had one arm slung around Pepper's neck and her favorite blue stuffed elephant toy tucked into the crook of her opposite elbow. Every night when Rachel tucked Annie into bed, she wanted that fuzzy elephant tucked in alongside her.

Now she offered the elephant to Pepper, and the dog reverently grabbed hold of it with her gentle mouth.

"Pepper and my elephant both want to sleep in my bed," Annie said, as clear and loud as a bell.

Rachel, Ian and Elma all exchanged a glance. For a second, no one seemed to know how to respond. They'd waited so long for Annie to speak like this, and now that it was happening, they were too astounded to react.

Abby, on the other hand, had plenty to say. "If Pepper sleeps with Annie, then Salty needs to sleep with me."

Rachel glanced at Ian. There was no way the dog and cat duo were going to bed in their crate in the mudroom tonight. She could tell just by the look on Ian's face that he would give Annie whatever she wanted, now that she'd found her voice again.

"Of course Pepper can sleep on your bed, Annie. And Salty can sleep in your room too." Ian fell to his knees and held out his arms. "Now, come here. All four of you."

Abby and Annie buried their faces in his shoulders, while Pepper nudged her way between them, still toting the elephant in her mouth. Salty rubbed against Ian's knees, and Elma graciously refrained from commenting on the copious amounts of cat hair he shed onto Ian's dress pants.

Instead, the older woman crossed the room to wrap her arms around Rachel.

"What was that for?" Rachel asked. Her throat grew tight when Elma drew out the embrace, hugging her tight.

"Thank you," was all Elma said.

But it was enough—more, in fact, than Rachel had dared to expect.

Later that night, Ian crept into the kitchen in his pajamas and got two silver candlesticks down from the cabinet over the refrigerator.

He'd checked in on the twins to make sure the addition of Pepper and Salty hadn't caused chaos instead of a peaceful night's sleep. To his mild surprise, the dog and cat had made themselves at home with no perceptible fuss or drama. Salty's slender feline form was curled into a tight ball in the crook of Abby's neck.

On the opposite side of the room, Annie slept soundly in her pink ruffled bed with Pepper stretched out beside her. Something about the sight of the blue elephant toy tucked between them nearly put a lump in Ian's throat.

For the first time in a long, long while, he felt like he had his family back. It looked different than it had before. They'd been through so much, but he and his girls were finally coming out of the dark place where they'd been stuck for the past few months. There would surely be more bumps ahead, but they would handle them this time. Together—Annie, Abby, Elma and Ian.

And Rachel too.

She had been such an instrumental part of their healing. Ian wanted her to know how much he appreciated her. They needed to celebrate. In all the excitement surrounding bedtime, they'd barely had a chance to exchange two words. Once he'd gotten the pets settled in the twins' bedroom, read everyone a fairy tale and gone back downstairs, Elma and Rachel had both gone home. But there'd been too much excitement fizzing through Ian's veins for him to sleep.

He found a matchbook from the Main Street Grille tucked in the back of a drawer and used it to light two slender taper candles. Then he gathered an ice bucket and two champagne flutes from the china cabinet in the dining room along with a bottle of French champagne that had been sitting in the wine rack for longer than he could remember.

Once he'd gotten everything set up, he jammed a hand through his hair and tried to look at it through Rachel's eyes. Would she think that was too much? He'd had a celebration in mind, but his chosen accessories were undeniably romantic.

Too late now, he thought. *Go big or go home*.

They'd been dancing around their attraction to each other for weeks. At first, Ian had done his best to deny his feelings. He'd fought them with everything he had. But he was so tired of bending over backward, trying not to feel anything. He was tired of seeking solace in numbness.

He wanted to feel. He wanted to *live*.

As the minutes ticked by and wax dripped down the candles, Ian thought perhaps Rachel wasn't coming. He hadn't specifically asked her to meet him here again. As Elma had pointed out, there was no more ice cream. No more pretense of the pets to check on. No reason at all, really, for either one of them to get out of bed and tiptoe into the dark kitchen.

But just as he bent his head to blow out the first candle, the back door opened, ever so slowly. All Ian's breath bottled up in his chest as he looked up and saw Rachel standing in the doorway in her delicate nightgown. Her hair blazed red in the moonlight, and her porcelain skin looked almost silver, as if she'd been dipped in stardust. She was so beautiful, inside and out.

When she stepped inside and closed the door behind her, the glow from the candles created a soft halo around her face. Light flickered and danced across the pale satin fabric of her gown.

"I wasn't sure if you'd be here," she said quietly. "There's no ice cream."

"Or dogs," Ian said, voice strained with longing.

"Or cats," she whispered, stepping closer…and closer…close enough for him to see the gentle parting of her lips. The boom of her pulse in the graceful hollow of her throat.

"Just you and me," he murmured, and it almost sounded like a promise. Because he meant it as one.

They could do this. He and Rachel could make this work. They could make each other happy. Ian was certain of it. He'd turned the idea over in his mind so many times, spending hour upon hour trying to convince himself that it was a bad idea. But he was ready to surrender. There wasn't a thought in his head as he and Rachel stood facing one another in the candlelight. Just want…and need…and a desire so profound that it nearly dragged him to his knees.

In the end, he wasn't sure who kissed who first. They moved toward each other in an instant, meeting someplace in the middle in a flurry of hands and sighs and breathy whispers.

Then finally—*finally*—their lips met.

And at long last, Ian Parsons was numb no longer.

Chapter Thirteen

The following morning, Ian cut his run short, having a mind to sneak into the kitchen and surprise Rachel while she got breakfast ready for the girls. He wanted to slide behind her, wrap his arms around her waist and press tender kisses to her neck until she melted into him the way she had last night.

They'd made out like two teenagers, almost until the sun came up. He should be exhausted right now, but instead, as his feet pounded against the pavement of Kingdom Creek's winding streets, he moved on pure adrenaline. And maybe something else—something he was hesitant to name, lest he scare Rachel off.

She hadn't seemed at all hesitant last night, though. Whatever he'd been feeling the past few weeks, she'd been experiencing it too. She hadn't told him as much, but she'd shown him with each tender caress, each touch of her lips, each breathy sigh he'd drawn out of her. Ian had never experienced a kiss like it.

Not even close.

He ate up the pavement on the way back home, anticipation tangling low in his gut. He needed to see her again before the day spun away from him and they were left with only snippets of time together in between kids and pets and his nosy but well-meaning mother-in-law.

He was too late, though. When he pushed the door open, it was Elma who greeted him with a half-empty coffee cup already in hand, not Rachel.

"Good morning, Ian." Elma looked him up and down. "Look at you. You've hardly broken a sweat."

"Yeah, um. I didn't feel much like running today." He shifted his weight from one foot to the other.

Elma arched an eyebrow. "Aren't you going to tell me good morning?"

"Yes. Sorry." He went to kiss her cheek. "Good morning, Elma."

He drew back just as Rachel walked into the room from the direction of the pantry, a box of confectioner's sugar in one hand and a small bag of flour in the other. She wore a frilly apron over her clothes, decorated with a cupcake print and a profusion of ruffles. Ian had never seen the apron before. It must have come from her modest collection of personal belongings stashed at the carriage house.

"Oh." Her cheeks went as pink as the ruffled trim of her apron, and her gaze went hot as their eyes met. "Hi, there."

"Hi, there," he said. His tone of voice alone probably gave them away. Those two short words somehow came out sounding far more intimate than he'd intended.

Elma glanced back and forth between them, frowning.

Rachel cleared her throat and nodded toward the kitchen counter where a collection of ingredients surrounded the standing mixer that Ian had forgotten he even owned. "I thought it would be nice to make cupcakes with the girls this morning. It seems like a good time to celebrate."

Ian nodded. "The perfect time."

Elma's frown deepened. "Why do I feel invisible all of a sudden?"

Rachel laughed and brushed past Ian in a fragrant cloud of spun sugar. "Don't be silly. Of course you're not invisible. Ian, Elma came by this morning to drop off some chicken tetrazzini as a thank-you for dinner-and-game night last night. Isn't that nice?"

"So nice." Even the prospect of one of his least favorite casseroles couldn't dampen his spirits. Not today. "Thank you, Elma."

"You're welcome," Elma said, but there was a wariness in her tone that Ian didn't care for.

Rachel wiped her hands on her apron and then planted them on her hips. "I'm going to go get the girls up. I'm pretty sure I heard the pitter-patter of puppy feet up there a few minutes ago. Pepper probably needs to go outside. I thought I'd take everyone to the park today for a little picnic. Maybe even a tea party."

"Annie and Abby would love that," Ian said.

"Super. I'll be right back." Rachel shot him a million-watt smile and practically floated toward the stairs.

Elma stared after her. Once she was out of view, Elma slowly turned toward Ian.

"What's going on?" she demanded.

Ian moved past her to reach for a coffee cup. He didn't want to have this conversation yet. Not like this. He hadn't had a chance to tell Rachel how he felt about her, and she certainly deserved to know before his mother-in-law did.

"Nothing," he said.

"That didn't look like nothing." She crossed her arms. "It very much seemed like…*something*."

"Elma, I assure you there's nothing to worry

about." Ian sipped from his mug. Was it too late to add a shot of whiskey to his coffee?

Elma harrumphed and narrowed her gaze at him, as if she could peer straight inside his head. "We don't actually know that much about Rachel, do we?"

Not this again. Just last night, she seemed to think Rachel had hung the moon.

"Rachel is a good person," Ian said. "End of story."

"Do you know where she was born?"

"No. Do you know where *I* was born?" he countered.

"Of course I do. You were born in Raleigh." Elma pursed her lips in triumph.

He should have known not to try and best her at her own game. While he didn't recall ever mentioning his birthplace to her before, she'd probably had a full background check run on him when he'd started dating Serena. "Regardless, where she was born doesn't matter."

"Except for the fact that her background is still rather vague." Elma snatched her purse from the kitchen table. "I think I'll do a little investigating."

Ian plunked his mug down. Coffee sloshed over the rim. "No, you won't."

"If she's such an angel, what harm could come from it?"

"It's not right." He shook his head. "It's an invasion of privacy, for starters."

"But you're her employer. Surely it's normal to do a cursory background check." Elma regarded him through narrowed eyes again. "Unless there's more going on here than a simple employment arrangement."

"Elma." Ian dragged a hand through his hair. What now? "Just don't, okay?"

She marched toward the door, shoulders squared. "We'll see. I'm not making any promises."

"For the record, I don't care for chicken tetrazzini," he muttered.

But she'd already slammed the door behind her.

As soon as the cupcakes were cooled and frosted, Rachel headed to the park with the girls. On the way, Pepper hung her head out of the car window, prompting giggles from the twins when the wind blew her ears back. Upon their arrival, the big Lab sat calmly in a fluffy pink tutu while they set up their tea party on a picnic blanket.

"My goodness, is that Pepper?" an older woman asked as she paused near the edge of the blanket.

She wore a T-shirt with the Furever Paws logo stitched above the pocket. A shaggy dog with a mop of white fur tugged at the end of the leash in her hand.

"It sure is." Rachel smiled as Pepper's tail began

to wag wildly. "Look, I think she remembers you. You're not Birdie Whitaker, are you?"

She had to be. She fit Ian's description of Bunny Whitaker's animal-saving sister to a T.

"I sure am." Birdie held out her hand for a shake. "You must be Rachel. Bunny told me all about you, Ian and the twins."

Rachel winced. "So I guess you heard we lost Annie for a few minutes."

Birdie shook her head. "That's not the way I heard it at all. From what Bunny told me, Annie ended up right where she belonged." She gave Pepper a pat on the head. "With Pepper here."

"True," Rachel said. She still felt terrible about letting Annie sneak out of her sight, but in the end, things had definitely worked out for the best. Thank goodness. "Would you like to join us for a cupcake?"

Pepper's entire canine face lit up as the twins began arranging cupcakes on a platter. The dog's tongue lolled out of the side of her mouth, as pink as the tutu tied around her midsection.

Birdie laughed. "No, thank you. You look like you have your hands full. Besides, I'm here to walk Marshmallow and practice a little training. I'm pitching in today because we're short-staffed at the shelter. We've been working on Marshmallow's *stay* command."

The shaggy white dog rolled a perfect somersault at the end of the leash. She hadn't managed to sit still for longer than a second since Rachel and Birdie had begun to chat.

"She seems a little antsy," Rachel said.

Birdie shrugged. "Stay is especially hard for some dogs, but it's one of the most important commands. In some situations, it can quite literally save a dog's life. Marshmallow has a tendency to bolt when she sees an open door. We're hoping to fix that before she gets adopted."

"How, exactly?"

"Time, practice and a lot of patience, along with loads of positive reinforcement. Eventually, it all just clicks." Birdie winked at Marshmallow. "One of these days, you'll realize that the best and safest place to be is right where you are."

Delighted to be the topic of conversation, Marshmallow hopped to her feet and trotted toward Rachel, who ran her fingers over the dog's soft fur. "You can do it, Marshmallow. I believe in you."

"Miss Rachel, I dropped one of the cupcakes!" Abby plucked a cupcake off the ground as tears filled her eyes.

"Oopsie. It's okay, sweetheart. We've got plenty," Rachel said.

"I'll let you get back to the girls. It was nice to meet you." Birdie pressed a hand to her heart. "And it was really nice to see Pepper so happy with her new family."

"Bye-bye." Annie waved one of her tiny hands.

Birdie waved back at her. "Bye-bye, sweetie."

Rachel bid farewell to the older woman as she scooped Abby into her arms. Once they'd practiced counting all the remaining cupcakes, the dropped one was quickly forgotten. The three of them went back to setting up the tea party.

Just as Rachel was walking to a nearby trash can with the discarded cupcake, she heard someone calling her name.

"Rachel?" A woman waved her arms from across the leafy park. "Rachel, is that you?"

Rachel pressed a palm to her thundering heart. She probably shouldn't have been so worried about someone recognizing her, considering she'd been in Spring Forest for weeks now. She had friends here. Of course she'd eventually run into people she knew while out and about.

Still, hearing her name like that when she wasn't expecting it made her feel like the rug was being swept out from under her. Chatting with Birdie was one thing, but being caught off guard by someone she couldn't see right away was another matter entirely. Someone was interested in *her*, not Pepper. And they knew her name.

Rachel's chest grew tight and she couldn't take

a full inhale until the woman drew closer and she realized who it was.

"Marianne?" *Calm down. It's just your old boss from the day care center. Nothing whatsoever to worry about.* She gulped in a lungful of air. "Sorry. You startled me."

The day school was just a block away, so Rachel really shouldn't have been so alarmed. Thankfully, Marianne didn't seem to notice how scared she'd been.

"I thought that was you!" Marianne leaned in and wrapped her arms around Rachel like they were old friends instead of just a former boss and employee. But that's simply how people were in Spring Forest. It wasn't just a town. It was a *community.* "Are you here with the Parsons twins?"

"Yes. And with Pepper, the new family dog. Ian adopted her from Furever Paws." Rachel glanced toward the shady spot nearby where Abby poured pretend tea into their teacups and Annie offered Pepper a dog biscuit on a tiny plastic plate.

The girls had wanted a "fancy" tea party, so they were both wearing flower crowns made from silk blossoms and long satin ribbons from their dress-up closet. Rachel had ironed their matching dresses with the Peter Pan collars. Of course Pepper had been dressed for the occasion with a fluffy tutu around her midsection.

"Well, if that isn't the most precious thing I've ever seen…" Marianne gasped. She watched the tea party closely for a second or two and then turned back to Rachel with an approving gleam in her eyes. "It looks like you've done wonders with Annie and Abby. I'm impressed."

"It's not just me. The dog has really helped Annie come out of her shell. And Ian…" Just saying his name made her feel like she was right back in his arms with his mouth moving against hers. So warm…so *right*. She cleared her throat. "I mean, Mr. Parsons… He's been amazing. Really, really great."

Marianne's lips curved into a knowing smile. "Has he, now?"

"With the girls," Rachel said, for clarity. Even so, her face grew warm. She knew that she was probably blushing as pink as the little bouquet of hand-picked roses that the twins had propped in a vase in the center of their picnic.

"You know, I sensed something between you and Ian Parsons back on the very first day the two of you met," Marianne said, eyes bright with curiosity.

"You did?" That couldn't be true, could it?

"Yes. Definitely."

"Well, it's not like that," Rachel heard herself say, as if by rote.

Her relationship with Ian wasn't really any of Marianne's business, and how was Rachel supposed to explain it when she didn't fully understand it herself?

They'd become more than friends—certainly more than employer and employee. The feelings she had for Ian were like nothing she'd ever experienced before. He was special…

Rachel had no idea how she was going to tell him goodbye when the time came.

"If there really is nothing there, then that's a shame." Marianne sighed. "You definitely have a special touch with his girls. That poor family has been through a lot. You came along just at the right time."

Rachel shook her head. As much as she wanted to cling to Marianne's words and hold them tight, she couldn't. If she did, she'd never be able to walk away with her heart in one piece. "It wasn't me. Time heals all wounds."

Marianne reached to squeeze Rachel's hand. "Surely you don't believe that. Just look at Annie and Abby. *Really* look."

Rachel glanced toward the picnic blanket spread beneath the limbs of the big tree, dripping with moss. Annie and Abby chattered away while Pepper's big head swiveled back and forth between the two. Annie bit into one of the cupcakes they'd made together that morning, and a daub of pink frosting clung to the tip of her pert nose. Pepper craned her neck and licked it off. Both girls collapsed into giggles.

"Could you imagine this scene taking place just a few weeks ago?" Marianne arched an eyebrow.

Rachel's throat squeezed closed. She was right. So much had changed. Rachel knew she couldn't take all the credit. It had been a team effort.

But she'd been a part of that team—a big part. And she wasn't ready to give the rest of them up. She had a feeling that she never would be.

She shook her head, as if doing so could somehow change her circumstances and make everything all sparkly and perfect, like shaking a glitter-filled snow globe. "But I'm not staying in Spring Forest. This was all just supposed to be temporary. The girls are going back to school. It's important for them to be around other children."

Marianne's forehead crinkled. "Oh, no. That's a shame. We're looking forward to the girls coming back to Spring Forest Day School, but they'll miss you terribly. I assumed you'd be staying on as their nanny."

Rachel nodded. "Yes, I suppose it is a shame."

Her voice cracked midsentence, and Marianne's gaze narrowed.

"Do you really have to go? Have you taken another job someplace else? Do you have family waiting for you back home somewhere?"

Of course not. Rachel had no one outside Spring Forest. No family, no friends, no home.

Just here. Just Ian and the twins.

She shook her head. If she tried to say it out loud, she would break down, and she didn't want the girls to look over and see her cry.

"Oh, honey." Marianne's gaze softened, as if she understood perfectly well how and why Rachel had ended up in their small town and why Rachel had begged Marianne not to use her full name. Maybe she did understand. Maybe Rachel should have been completely honest from the beginning and shared more of herself with the people in her new life. Maybe she still could. "Then, why don't you stay?"

It wasn't too late, was it? She could still tell the truth. But would the truth really change things? The lid of Pandora's box worked both ways, didn't it? If she opened it up and let the truth out, her past could still come back to haunt her. No one could stop it. Not even Ian.

But maybe if it did, they could face it together. That wasn't such a pipe dream.

Was it?

Rachel took a deep breath. Just over Marianne's shoulder, she could see Annie and Abby chasing Pepper in circles around the picnic blanket. Just as they caught up with the big dog, she turned on a dime, ears flying and tail wagging. Then the game of chase spun into reverse, with the girls running and squealing as Pepper pranced at their heels.

That's it, Rachel thought. *That's the only sort of running I want in my life now.*

No more hiding, no more fear. Just sunshine and laughter. Flower crowns and puppy antics. Midnight ice cream sundaes and tender kisses with the best, most wonderful man she'd ever known. They could take the girls to see the Doggy Fashion Show.

They could be a family.

Birdie's words echoed in the back of her head, as if they'd been meant for her instead of Marshmallow.

One of these days you'll realize that the best and safest place to be is right where you are.

A chill ran up and down Rachel's spine. If she didn't know better, she'd be tempted to think that the Whitaker sisters were some sort of pet-saving fairy godmother duo.

"Maybe I will." She felt herself smile. "Maybe I'll stay."

The intercom on Ian's phone buzzed, dragging his attention away from the PowerPoint presentation he'd been working on all morning and afternoon.

His assistant's voice blared from the speaker. "Mr. Parsons, you have a visitor."

Ian sighed. He was so close to finishing the presentation. Just a few more slides to go. If he kept his head down, he could probably get out of the office by five and home in time to help Rachel with dinner and give the twins their baths. But such a plan left no time for a meeting, particularly an unexpected one.

He picked up the phone. "I don't have anything on my calendar for this afternoon."

"I know. It's a drop-in. I tried to tell her you were busy…" The assistant cleared his throat. "Several times, in fact. But she insisted, and now she says she's not leaving until she has a chance to speak with you."

"It's an emergency," someone in the background said. "Tell him that I need to speak with him right now."

Ian squeezed his eyes shut. *Elma.* He'd recognize the sound of that voice anywhere.

So she was interrupting him at work now? Ian had thought things between them had been getting better. Their relationship certainly still had room for improvement, but it had gotten better in recent weeks. He'd been more welcoming with her, and she, in turn, had become a little less intrusive and clingy. He'd thought so, anyway.

Something must have been terribly wrong for her to show up at his office, though. Elma had never set foot in his workplace before.

Ian leaned closer to the phone. "Go ahead and send her in."

He prayed something wasn't wrong with the girls…the house…Rachel. Surely if a tragedy or something truly terrible had happened, he'd have gotten a call from the police or the hospital.

He stood up, raked a hand through his hair and tried not to panic. Then his assistant opened the door to usher Elma inside the office and the knot in Ian's gut hardened into irritation. Her pursed lips and squared shoulders immediately told him that she hadn't barged into his workday because some sort of harm had come to his family.

She was here for another reason entirely. She didn't look worried or frightened. She looked self-righteous and indignant.

What in the world had he done wrong now? For the life of him, he had no idea.

"Elma," he said as politely and patiently as he could manage. "This is a surprise."

She plopped down into one of the chairs on the opposite side of his desk. "Is it always so difficult to get in to see you? I've been waiting for fifteen minutes. What if I'd been a client?"

"You're not a client, though."

"No, I'm not. I'm *family*, which is even more important than business." Elma tutted.

Ian was already beginning to lose track of whatever point she was trying to make. He took a deep breath and held up his hands, as if trying to calm an unruly child. "Let's start over again. Clearly, you're upset."

"Of course I'm upset. You'll be upset, too, once I tell you what I came here to say." Elma's eyes shot sparks.

Ian's gut churned. He had a bad feeling about whatever was going on here. This went beyond Elma's usual complaints.

He crossed his arms and braced himself for whatever was coming. "Has something happened?"

"You'd better believe something happened." She leveled her gaze at him, eyes glittering with fury. "And that *something* is named Rachel Gray."

A muscle in Ian's jaw clenched. He had work to do. He was not going to stand there and listen to Serena's mother complain about Rachel again—especially now that he'd realized he had feelings for her. *Real* feelings. Feelings that went far beyond anything he'd ever expected when he'd all but begged her to come into their lives.

"Elma—" he started, but at the same time, his mother-in-law blurted out a sentence that left him completely and utterly speechless.

"There's no Rachel Gray in the Virginia educational accreditation system."

Ian sank into his chair as if he'd been sucker punched. Still, he knew there must be some mistake. "What are you talking about?"

"Don't you remember that first night she came to dinner?" Elma pressed her lips together, eyebrows raised.

"Of course I remember," Ian said quietly. That was the night everything had changed. It had been a turning point, whether he'd realized it or not at the time.

You knew. You knew from the moment you first set eyes on Rachel.

"She sat at the dining room table and told us she'd moved to Spring Forest from Virginia. She said she was an accredited child behavior specialist there, and she was waiting for her state credentials to come through in North Carolina," Elma said.

Ian knew all of this. How could he have forgotten? That paperwork was the axe waiting to fall on his head. Every single day he worried Rachel would come to him and say she'd gotten her state credentials and it was time for her to move on to another job—the sort of job she'd trained for. And every day he felt guilty about wishing and hoping for more time.

They'd moved past this, though, hadn't they? The kiss had changed things. He and Rachel hadn't had a chance to actually sit down and talk about it yet, but she had to know how he felt about her. He didn't care if she wanted to work someplace else, but he didn't want her to leave. His home was her home.

Or so he'd thought.

"She *is* an accredited child specialist," Ian said. It was true. It *had* to be true. He'd trusted her with his children. Rachel didn't like to talk about her past, and he'd accepted that.

But she wasn't the type of person to misrepresent her qualifications—with good reason. He'd brought her into his home as the nanny for his girls during a time when they needed special care. Being anything less than truthful about her background in childcare would be a serious problem.

"No, she's not." Elma dug around in her purse and pulled out a folded sheet of paper. "Here. See for yourself."

The paper shook ever so slightly in Ian's hands as he scanned the letterhead at the top of the page. *The Virginia Department of Education.* It certainly looked official. Ian knew Elma would never forge a government letter, anyway. She could be frustrating from time to time—overbearing, even—but Ian knew he could trust her to be honest.

Just like he knew he could trust Rachel.

Can you, though?

He sat up straighter, doing his best to steady himself so he could concentrate on the short letter in his hands. But the moment he read the first paragraph, the bottom dropped out of his cozy new world.

Dear Mrs. Miller,
Thank you for your inquiry about a child be-
havior specialist in the state of Virginia. Unfor-
tunately, there isn't an individual by the name
of Rachel Gray in our records. Nor can we lo-
cate a person with that name in our archives.

Ian could barely absorb the words on the page.
He felt like he was reading about a completely different person than the Rachel he knew and loved...

There was no other word for the feelings he had
for her—*love.* He was in love with her. Admitting
it to himself felt monumental. But also bittersweet,
because if she wasn't the person he thought she was,
then who exactly was she?

His head spun with such ferocity that he could
barely get through the rest of the letter.

Misrepresenting state qualifications is a
crime—one that we take very seriously. If you
are aware of an individual presenting fraudu-
lent certification from the state board, please
contact us with additional information.
Very sincerely...

Ian's head snapped up to meet Elma's gaze.
"You're not actually going to try and have her ar-
rested, are you?"

There had to be a reasonable explanation. The Department of Education had made a mistake, that's all. Or he and Elma had misheard when Rachel mentioned she was certified in Virginia. Maybe she meant West Virginia—or somewhere else entirely.

Both of you misheard? Not likely.

He needed to get out of there. He needed to see Rachel in person and get to the bottom of this horrible misunderstanding. But first, he wanted to make sure Elma hadn't gone completely off the deep end and reported the woman he loved to the authorities.

Ian stared hard at Elma, with his heart in his throat and vulnerability seeping from his every pore. If his mother-in-law hadn't yet realized how much Rachel meant to him, she definitely did now. The truth was probably written all over his face.

Truth. What did that word even mean? He'd thought he knew—before his world had turned upside down mere seconds ago.

"No, of course I'm not going to report her to the police," Elma finally said. Her gaze dropped to her lap, as if looking him in the eye and seeing what this unwelcome news was doing to him was too agonizing to bear. "I don't think she's a *criminal*. I just…"

Elma sighed, and she seemed to age ten years right before Ian's eyes. The pain of losing her daughter was etched in every deep crease on her forehead and the lines that pulled her mouth into a perpetual frown. And when she lifted her eyes back to his, the grief he saw looking back at him was an ache he knew all too well.

"I wasn't going to let anyone walk off the street and into our lives and take my daughter's place. I couldn't do that, Ian." A lone tear slipped down Elma's cheek.

He reached into his desk drawer for a handkerchief and handed it to her. "No one will ever take Serena's place, Elma. That's not what this was about."

Was...

Past tense. Because unless there was an innocent explanation—which was beginning to seem increasingly unlikely—he and Rachel weren't coming back from this. If she'd lied to him about anything else, it would have been okay. But it was on the basis of her qualifications that he'd brought her into his home to look after his children. Annie and Abby were too precious. They were everything to him, and he would lay down his life to protect them. How could he have left them in the hands of a total stranger?

Because if Rachel had lied to him about her qualifications, that's what she was. A stranger—certainly not the love of his life, no matter how much it might feel that way.

"I don't know, Ian. Without Serena here, sometimes I feel so lost that I don't know much of any-

thing anymore. But one thing I know for certain…"
Elma offered him a smile so sad that he felt it in the
deepest part of his bones. "Rachel isn't who you
think she is."

Chapter Fourteen

Rachel knew something was wrong the moment Ian walked through the door.

He'd been planning on coming home early enough to have dinner with the twins and have a little family time before they had to go to bed. Rachel knew he had a big presentation he was working on at the office, so she wasn't entirely surprised when he texted to let her know he wasn't going to make it. Deadlines were deadlines, after all.

But his message seemed terser than the other texts he normally sent her when he needed to check in with the girls or when he wanted to let her know he was running late. Those messages normally included an emoji or two. Sometimes he told her to give Abby and Annie a kiss or a hug from him. Once, he'd even sent a funny video for her to play for them.

This time, his text had been brief and to the point.

Working late.

Rachel had done her best not to read too much into it. Clearly, he was busy with the presentation, and he didn't have time to send a chatty message or a cute video.

It was the kiss... That kiss had changed everything. Maybe Rachel had just been fooling herself. To some people, a kiss was just a kiss. But not to her—especially after everything she'd been through. A few months ago, she would have said she'd never kiss a man ever again. She couldn't imagine even wanting to.

But getting to know Ian had changed things. He'd brought her back to life after a time of terrible darkness, by giving her back the one thing she'd given up a long time ago—hope.

She'd forgotten what it was like to believe that life could be wonderful and joyful. She'd forgotten what it was like to feel butterflies in her belly when someone walked into the room. She'd definitely forgotten how sweet a kiss could be. There'd been a tenderness in Ian's lips, in his hands, in his touch—a reverence that told in no uncertain terms that he didn't want to break her.

On the contrary, Rachel felt like Ian Parsons had come into her life to help her put herself back together again.

How could he possibly know that, though? She hadn't breathed a word to him about her past. In the beginning, it had been a simple matter of self-preservation. And then, before long, it seemed to be far too late to change course and tell him the truth.

She had to, though—especially now that she'd decided to stay in Spring Forest. If she was going to make her home here, a real home, she needed to be honest and up-front about everything. Rachel couldn't let another day pass without coming clean. She didn't know how she was going to tell Ian. She just knew she had to.

Tonight.

But as soon as her gaze met Ian's and she took in the deep black of his irises and the hard set of his jaw, her determination wavered. She hadn't been reading too much into the curtness of his text message. He was obviously upset.

No. Rachel's stomach churned. *He's more than upset. He's angry. At me.*

Her breathing went instantly shallow as every cell in her body went on high alert. Fight-or-flight response—that's what her therapist back in Virginia had called it. Rachel didn't want to do either of those things, though. They sounded equally terrible. The last thing she wanted to do was fight with Ian, but running away would be just as heartbreaking.

She swallowed hard and reminded herself that just because her body had gone into panic mode didn't mean there was actually something to be afraid of. This was the same man who'd kissed her silly last night—the same one who she knew with every fiber of her being would never do anything to hurt her.

"Ian, hi," she said through a shaky inhale. "It's so late. I'm sure you're glad to be home."

He nodded and tugged at the knot in his tie. "Something came up this afternoon, and afterward, it was a struggle to finish the presentation."

He looked away and couldn't seem to meet her gaze.

"That's too bad. The girls are fine, though, all tucked into bed with Pepper and Salty. I promised them I'd tell you they said good-night." Rachel crossed her arms and promptly uncrossed them again, brimming with nervous energy.

Just tell him. Tell him now, and get it over with.

The timing wasn't ideal, but Rachel knew she'd lose her nerve if she didn't get it out as soon as possible. She should have never kissed him without telling him her whole story.

"Listen, we need to talk," Ian said, as if he'd plucked the words straight out of her brain.

Rachel nodded. "Of course. I've been wanting to talk to you, actually. I—"

"Who are you?" Ian said without bothering to let her finish.

Her knees buckled, and she grabbed on to the kitchen counter to steady herself. He couldn't know, could he?

No, it wasn't possible.

Then why is he looking at you like you're a complete stranger?

"Ian, I'm not sure what you're asking me," she said. Another lie. Why couldn't she just tell him the truth?

"Let's see if I can make it clearer." He sat down at the kitchen table—the same place where they'd been having secret ice cream dates for over a week now. The same place where he'd looked at her with eyes filled with longing and promises that neither one of them had been able to bring themselves to utter out loud.

Not here, she wanted to say. She loved this old table. Everything that had happened between them, everything that had led up to last night's kiss had happened in this very spot. The grooves and swirls

in the smooth wooden surface held their secrets—
the midnight whispers, the loaded glances, the
gradual shift in their relationship from friends to
something more. Something special. She didn't want
it to be the place where it all fell apart.

"You told me you were waiting for your certification to come through from the state of Virginia, did
you not?" Ian raised a brow. A challenge.

She gave him a firm nod. That part was true at
least. "Yes, I did."

"Then, why does the Virginia State Board of Education say that they've never licensed a child behavioral specialist by the name of Rachel Gray?" For
the first time since he'd come home, the sharp edge
in his voice softened, and the ache in its place made
Rachel want to weep.

Of course he'd checked up on her credentials. She
had no right whatsoever to be upset about it, either.
He'd hired her to look after his children. Verify-
ing her qualifications was completely natural and
expected.

Which was precisely why she'd never intended to
tell anyone about her certification, outside of Marianne. When Marianne hired her, it had felt like a
miracle from heaven, especially when she'd agreed
to call Rachel by her first and middle name only,
no questions asked.

But when Ian first invited Rachel over and asked

for her help with the girls, Elma had been so leery. Rachel had simply wanted to put the twins' grandmother at ease, so she'd let her true qualifications slip.

And now Ian was looking at her like she'd just kicked a puppy.

"I can explain." Rachel sat down across from him. She didn't bother mentioning that she'd been about to tell him the truth. Why would he believe her, now that she'd just been proved a liar? "I promise."

The tiniest spark of hope flashed in Ian's eyes, and Rachel could almost breathe again—emphasis on *almost*. Perhaps all wasn't lost, after all.

"I'm listening," Ian said.

His gaze might have softened, but his voice remained stiff and detached. Rachel hadn't heard Ian sound quite like this since the day they'd collided into one another at the preschool and sent little wooden alphabet blocks tumbling in every direction.

It sort of felt like those same blocks were knocking around in her rib cage right now. But that was just her heart—broken, battered and, once again, bracing itself for the worst.

"I really am a child behavior specialist, licensed in the state of Virginia. I would never lie about something like that. I hope you believe me." She *needed* him to believe. More than anything. "When I spoke to you that first day and said that I could help, I knew that I had the training and experience to make that happen. And I'm so glad it has. I've loved working with Abby and Annie. The girls mean the world to me… So do you."

Her fingertips inched toward his across the table-top, but she stopped short of touching him. Once she dropped the bomb, she was worried he'd pull away, and she wouldn't be able to bear it if that happened. So with their hands just a whisper apart, she took a deep breath and told him the truth.

"My name isn't really Rachel Gray."

Ian stared down at his hands.

Rachel's fingertips were right there, a fraction of an inch away, sparks of invisible electricity crackling between them, as always. He had to tamp down the urge to reach for her and weave his fingers through hers.

He missed her touch, missed the easy rapport that had developed between them, missed *her*. Because he didn't know the woman sitting across from him anymore. He never had, apparently.

My name isn't really Rachel Gray.

No matter how many times he turned her words over in his head, they didn't make sense. He closed his eyes, willing himself to wake up from this night-mare and find himself sitting at the kitchen in the middle of the night with an ice cream sundae in front of him, the comforting weight of Pepper's warm bulk on his feet and Rachel smiling across the table at him with a dollop of whipped cream on the tip her nose.

But when he opened his eyes, nothing had changed. He was still right there, watching his dreams of a brand-new life wither and die in the eyes of a woman he didn't recognize. At all.

"Although, I guess it would be more accurate to say my *full* name isn't Rachel Gray. My last name is Wilson." Her chin wobbled, and Ian averted his gaze. God help him if she actually cried. He wouldn't be able to stand it, no matter who she really was. "I'm Rachel Gray Wilson."

Ian snorted. "Well, that's a relief."

Was she serious? He'd let her into his home, trusted her with his *children*, and she'd been dishonest about the most basic information imaginable. What possible explanation could she give that would justify that?

He swiveled his gaze back toward her in a hard stare and slid his hands into his lap.

Rachel's fingertips fluttered, like the wings of a bird that didn't know where to land. Then she bit down hard on her bottom lip as she pulled her hands toward her and wrapped her arms around her middle. "I know you might doubt it, but I had a good reason for not sharing my entire name."

Ian said nothing and let the simple fact that he was still sitting there, still listening, speak for itself. If she'd been anyone else, he would've fired her on the spot.

"The reason I left Virginia was because I was involved in an abusive relationship." Rachel said the words so quietly that Ian almost didn't hear them. "I dated my boyfriend, Frank James, for two years."

Ian's hands clenched into fists in his lap. He wasn't sure he wanted to hear this. He was desperate to know the real Rachel and understand why she'd lied about her very identity, but the idea of someone hurting her made him sick to his stomach. And the thought of her with another man sent a burning sensation straight to his heart.

Because you love her...no matter what her last name is.

"Oh, Rachel." He shook his head. "I—"

She held up a hand. "Let me finish. Please. I just want to get the whole story out there, before I lose my nerve."

Ian nodded. "That's fair."

"Thank you." She blew out a tremulous breath. "Anyway, Frank and I started dating right around the holidays. Christmas has always been kind of a lonely time since my father passed away. It was always just us, since my mom died when I was just a baby. But it was still my favorite time of year, and once he was gone… I guess what I'm trying to say is that I was in an especially vulnerable place. And then I met Frank."

She gave him a sad smile, and Ian felt her shame and embarrassment all the way down to his marrow. He had to bite his tongue to honor her wishes and keep his mouth shut. He wanted desperately to tell her she had nothing to be ashamed of, but he would have to wait until she'd finished. If anyone knew what it felt like to be lost and blinded by grief and loneliness, it was Ian.

"In retrospect, I can see how controlling he was, right at the start. But at the time, I mistook his intense interest in every part of my life for affection. It feels pathetic to say this out loud, but it was nice to have someone care about where I went or who I was with."

Ian shook his head. It wasn't pathetic. It was heartbreaking. And anyway, who was he to judge how someone dealt with grief? He was a grown man who continually let his dead wife's mother cook all his meals. Ian was far from perfect. He'd had his own struggles, which was part of the reason he felt so protective of his girls. His family was the one thing he couldn't—*wouldn't*—screw up. And not just because he'd made a promise to Serena. Being a father was the most important role he had.

"He wanted to control me, and I thought…" She

let her voice drift off as her eyes filled with unshed tears. Then she shook her head and looked anywhere and everywhere besides at Ian. "...I thought he loved me. I couldn't have been more wrong. The control issue got worse, and by the time the emotional abuse started, I'd lost most of my close friends. I felt like I was as worthless as Frank told me I was. I didn't have anyone to talk to or anywhere to go."

"But you did." Ian swallowed hard. "You're here now, so you were able to end things."

Thank God she'd managed to walk away. He still wasn't entirely sure how her fake name entered the picture, though.

She nodded. "I did, yes. After he hit me for the first time, I knew I had to find a way."

"He *hit* you?" A jolt of white-hot fury shot through Ian, and before he knew what he was doing, he'd flown to his feet. The chair he'd been sitting in skittered across the hardwood floor, and Rachel flinched.

A guilty knot formed at the back of his throat when he realized he'd frightened her. Suddenly, so many things made sense—Rachel's reluctance to answer his questions when he'd first sought her opinion at the preschool, her meager possessions, her safety concerns about the carriage house. She hadn't simply broken things off with that monster.

She'd fled.

"Ian, can you sit back down?" She looked up at him, her eyes huge in her face. "Please?"

"Yes," he said as evenly as possible. "Yes, of course. I'm sorry. I didn't mean to...to startle you." *To scare you.* "I just... This is a lot to take in."

He wanted to find this Frank James character and pummel the guy. Rachel was gentle and kind. What sort of man would hurt someone like that? No woman deserved to experience that sort of cruelty, obviously, but it was especially hard to believe anyone could lash out at someone so wonderful. Ian just couldn't wrap his head around a man actually striking Rachel or telling her she was worthless.

"When I told Frank I didn't want to see him anymore, the violence escalated. He told me if I ever left him, he'd find me and he'd kill me." She frowned and got a faraway look in her eyes. "It was only six months ago that I left, but it almost feels like a lifetime. Like all those terrible things happened to another person."

"Six months." Ian took a sharp inhale. Six months was nothing in the grand scheme of things. Her ex could still be searching for her.

"I left in the middle of the night. I just packed what I could fit into a suitcase and took off on a Greyhound bus. I dropped my last name so he wouldn't be able to find me. Since then, I've been moving from town to town, not staying anyplace long enough for him to track me down and taking on small jobs where I wouldn't have to use my state certification. If I took a job within the system, he'd be able to locate me in an instant." Rachel's arms tightened around her, as if it was taking every shred of strength she had left simply to hold herself together.

Ian nodded. If Elma had known Rachel's real last name, it would have been easy as pie to get an update from the Virginia Department of Education. The letter she'd wielded at his office earlier proved that much.

"So that's why I lied about my name. And that's why I insisted on taking this job on a temporary basis." Rachel lifted her gaze to his, and beyond the veil of tears, her eyes looked greener than ever. Like lush spring grass after a rainstorm. "I'd actually been planning on talking to you about that tonight...about staying."

Ian's heart stuttered in his chest. She wanted to stay?

It was the news Ian had been desperate to hear for weeks—especially once things had changed between them. Once he'd realized he'd fallen in love.

But right now, his thoughts were a blur of desire, shock and a thousand other emotions. He was feeling everything at once, all the emotions he'd tried so hard to keep at bay since Serena died. He'd allowed himself to be so numb for so long that he didn't know how to process such intense human feelings anymore. He was like poor Pepper and Salty had been back at Furever Paws, hiding in the back corner of their shared kennel. Desperate for connection, but too comfortable in the darkness to venture into the light.

Until the right person came along.

Ian watched as a lone tear slid down Rachel's cheek. Was she still the right person? His heart and soul said yes, but his mind had snagged on one nagging detail from her story.

He tilted his head as dread pooled low in his belly. He didn't want to ask the question, but he had to. "How did you know Frank wouldn't find you here if you chose to stay?"

Rachel blinked. "I didn't. I still don't, technically. I just—I can't keep running. I don't want to run anymore. I want to stay here with the girls…with *you*."

Her words should have been music in his ears, but his Papa Bear instincts kicked into high gear, obliterating every last shred of his common sense. Just like they'd done at the preschool when he and Rachel had first met.

"So you took this job, knowing the entire time that your dangerous ex might track you down…that he could have come here while you were home alone with Abby and Annie?"

Ian wanted to reel the words back in the moment

they'd left his mouth. He hadn't realized how awful they'd sound until they were out in the open—like he was blaming her for all that had happened to her, which was the last thing he'd wanted to do.

Worst of all was seeing the words hit her like a blow. She physically flinched at the idea that she might have put Abby and Annie in danger. "Um, I suppose that's true," she said. "I hadn't thought about it that way before, but you're right. Just by being here, I put your children in danger." Rachel's face crumpled.

She stood, and when he rose to his feet to wrap his arms around her and apologize, she backed away. She began crying in earnest, hot tears spilling down her beautiful face. He wanted to kiss them away, one by one, but he didn't dare make another move to touch her. That wasn't what Rachel wanted.

It hadn't been the cruel man from her past who'd caused the tears this time.

It had been Ian.

Chapter Fifteen

"Can we have another tea party in the park today?" Annie blinked sleepy eyes up at Rachel the following morning as she padded into the kitchen in her favorite footie pajamas. The flower crown from yesterday was sitting crooked atop her head, and as usual, Pepper trotted at her side. "Please?"

Abby followed behind them with Salty cradled in her arms, whispering softly into one of the cat's dark ears. Rachel caught the words *tea party*, loud and clear.

"You know what? Why don't we have a tea party right here at home?" Rachel scooped pet food into Pepper's and Salty's respective bowls. "We can dec-

orate the garden out back and invite your grandmother. How does that sound?"

"Gammy." Annie nodded, and Pepper woofed
her approval.

"Great. I'll give her a call while you girls have
breakfast." Rachel made her best attempt at a smile.

It actually hurt, and not just because her skin
was tight and her eyes were puffy from crying. Last
night had been a complete disaster, and this morning hadn't been much of an improvement. Ian had
spoken politely to her before he'd left for the office,
but things between them just weren't the same.

They never would be.

Rachel knew he hadn't meant to insinuate that
she'd intentionally put his family in danger. She'd
taken him by surprise with her story, and he'd just
reacted without thinking. Ian had apologized immediately. He'd tried to embrace her, and Rachel had almost let him. Maybe if she had, they would've fallen
back into the sweet, heady place they'd found, where
just the sound of his voice gave her butterflies—
where she'd felt treasured every time he touched her.

Rachel would never know if they could make
their way back to that special place of tenderness,
though. Because she couldn't let her guard down
again. It had been a mistake to do so the first time,
because Ian had been right—just by being here, in

his house, she was potentially putting Abby and Annie in harm's way.

The thought of Frank tracking her down and coming to this house terrified her more than any of the awful things she'd already experienced. It just couldn't happen. Rachel would rather give up her entire new life in Spring Forest than cause Abby and Annie to experience any more trauma.

So that's exactly what she was going to do—give it up.

"Pepper, let Mr. Salty eat his breakfast," Rachel said in the same singsong voice she used every morning when the Lab tried to sneak over to Salty's bowl after she'd gobbled up her kibble.

As usual, Pepper reversed course and trotted toward the table to sit beneath Annie's chair while she finished the scrambled eggs and cinnamon toast on her *Angelina Ballerina* plate.

The scene was the same as it was every morning. Rachel, the twins, the dog and the cat had developed a familiar breakfast ritual—an intentional act, on Rachel's part. Routines gave children a sense of stability and security. Knowing what to expect made them feel safe, especially children like Annie and Abby, whose lives had already been touched by tragedy at such a young age.

This morning *felt* different for Rachel, though. Because she knew it was the last one. There wouldn't be any more pigtailed twins in her future. No more *Angelina Ballerina* plates. No more rescue pets weaving through her legs or nudging her hand for a pat.

No more Ian.

"Miss Rachel sad?" Annie's forehead puckered and a sliver of toast dangled from her fingertips as she regarded Rachel.

"Oh, no, sweetheart." Rachel squatted down to Annie's eye level and grinned as hard as she could, despite the lump in her throat that felt as big as Pepper's jumbo-sized bag of dog food. "Why would I be sad? We're going to have a lovely day with your gammy."

"Miss Rachel sad," Abby said with the bluntness that only a toddler could muster.

"I'm just tired, that's all," Rachel said.

It wasn't a lie. She'd never felt so drained and exhausted in her life. That's what tossing and turning all night long did to a person. But no matter how much time she'd passed weighing the options in her head, no matter how many hours she'd spent staring at the ceiling through a blurry veil of tears, she hadn't been able to come up with another solution.

Rachel would just start over…again. A new job. A new town. A new life. That's what she needed, and this time, she wouldn't make the mistake of losing her heart to a precious family that would've been better off if she'd never come into their life. This was her new plan, and it sounded perfectly safe.

And perfectly lonely.

Rachel stood, turning her back on the girls and blinking hard. She wasn't sure how she was going to get through the rest of the day.

You can do it. Just get Elma here, and then you can leave. You'll be far away from Spring Forest before Ian even gets home from work.

"Okay, girls. Why don't you play with your blocks while I call Gammy Elma. In just a few minutes we can pick out something fun to wear for your tea party."

"Tea party!" Abby fist-punched the air as she slid out of her chair and skipped out of the kitchen. Salty paused from licking his paws, then darted after her in a streak of fawn-and-chocolate fur.

Annie and Pepper's exit was a bit more subdued as Annie removed her flower crown and tried to balance it on the dog's head while they walked in Abby and Salty's wake. The first time it fell to the ground, Annie scooped it up and placed it back on Pepper's head. After the second wobble, Pepper gingerly picked it up with her teeth. Annie shrugged, seemingly happy to let the dog carry the crown in her mouth instead of wearing it on her head.

Rachel's heart squeezed as Abby took Annie by the hand and they ran off to play.

Don't cry. And whatever you do, don't think about saying goodbye. Just call Elma and get ready for the tea party.

Rachel's suitcase was already packed in the carriage house. The sooner Elma could come over, the better.

"A tea party? That sounds nice," Elma said on the other end of the phone after Rachel had issued the invitation. "Thank you for inviting me."

Was Rachel imagining things, or did she sound a bit stilted? "Of course. The girls are excited to have you over. They made cupcakes the other day. Strawberry with pink frosting."

"What time shall I arrive?"

Rachel grew still. Elma's voice and her choice of words definitely seemed odd. Detached, almost. Definitely out of character for her ordinary, almost overbearing persona.

"In an hour? Does that work for you?" Rachel said, and as soon as Elma agreed and she'd ended the call, it dawned on her…

Elma knew that Rachel had lied to Ian.

Of course she knew. She had probably been the one who'd contacted the state of Virginia to verify Rachel's credentials. Ian had said that she always had to know everything about everyone. Of course she would look into the woman caring for her grandchildren. Everything was suddenly starting to make a lot more sense.

Not that it mattered. Rachel had made up her mind. She couldn't stay here, and her decision didn't have a thing to do with Elma. She was leaving to protect Annie and Abby.

If Elma already knew, all the better. It would make things simpler when Rachel told her she was leaving.

Who are you kidding? It's still going to be complicated.

Rachel couldn't think about that right now, though. She had a tea party to plan.

Ian couldn't concentrate on his presentation. The figures on the computer screen swam in front of his eyes. He blinked. Hard.

Get it together. You've been working on this for weeks.

His personal life was hanging by a thread, which really shouldn't have been anything new. Ian hadn't even had a personal life until recently. He hadn't even wanted one. But now…

Things had changed. For a bright, shining moment, he'd been himself again. The old Ian. He'd been happy. And now he'd gone and screwed things up.

Work was the only place where Ian had felt remotely competent for the past year. He couldn't ruin this part of his life too. The very least he could do was ensure that his daughters had a decent roof over their heads. He just needed to get through the day and present his work to the client without making another disaster of things. Then he could go home and try to make things right with Rachel.

His heart wasn't in his work, though. Neither was his head.

"Mr. Parsons, is there anything I can do to help?" Ian's assistant crossed her arms in front of his desk. He'd been so distracted that he hadn't even heard her enter his office.

How long had she been standing there watching him stare blankly at his computer screen?

"Thanks, but no." He blew out a breath and pushed his chair back from his desk. He needed some air. He needed caffeine. But what he needed most of all was hope.

Not that he'd manage to find that at the bottom of a coffee cup, but it was worth a shot. He couldn't keep sitting at his desk in a blind panic. Since the talk last night with Rachel, he wasn't sure if he'd managed to take a full breath. He felt like a tight band had wound itself around his chest, pressing all of his regret, all of his mistakes, deep inside. Squeezing out room for anything else.

"I'm going to go around the corner and grab some coffee," he said, reaching for his jacket.

Ian was wearing his best Armani suit and his favorite necktie. A power tie, the men's magazines probably would have called it. Hermès. Bright crimson silk. But that was not why it was Ian's favorite. This was the tie that Rachel had fashioned into a perfect Windsor knot for him back when she'd first started working as the twins' nanny. He couldn't look at it without imagining her delicate fingertips moving along the smooth silk, the way his heart had leaped straight to his throat as she rested her palm against his chest, the jolt of awareness he'd felt. So sudden and so strong that it had nearly knocked him flat on his back.

That was the moment this particular tie had become his favorite.

"But your presentation is in an hour." His assistant cast a worried glance at the clock on his credenza. "You don't have to leave. I'd be happy to go get the coffee for you."

"I've got it. I'll only take a moment," Ian said, and then he all but fled from the office, gasping for air.

He hadn't signed up for this. He'd been just fine before Rachel had come along.

Okay, that was a lie. He hadn't been fine, but he'd managed to breathe. He'd managed to get through the day with one foot in front of the other. And now he'd lost his sense of equilibrium. Up was down, and down was up. Nothing made sense without her.

He yanked open the door to the coffee shop and reached into his pocket for his cell phone. He tapped in Rachel's contact information, but the call rolled almost immediately to voice mail, just as it had done the previous three times he'd tried to call.

"Whoa, there." Harris Vega held up his hands as Ian nearly plowed straight into him. "Where's the fire?"

Ian took a step back.

"Sorry. I wasn't watching where I was going. I'm…" Lost. Completely and utterly lost. "Sorry."

He slipped his phone back in his pocket.

Harris tilted his head, studying Ian in a way that made him wonder if his troubles were written across his forehead for everyone to see. "Are you okay? You don't look so good."

Ian shifted from one foot to the other. He and Harris were casual acquaintances, not close friends. Ian didn't have much time for friends. That was what he'd told himself every time he turned down a social invitation, anyway. But maybe that was just another way of isolating himself from the world around him. Maybe it was time for that, too, to stop.

"I will be," Ian said. *Just as soon I talk to Rachel.*

"Okay." Harris nodded, took a sip from the paper coffee cup in his hand and didn't press for more information. No wonder everyone in town seemed to love this guy. He was a successful house flipper and as easygoing as they came. "Well, I'm always up for a coffee if you ever need to talk."

"Thanks. I might take you up on that sometime. I'd do it now, but I've got a meeting at the office at the top of the hour. And then there are some things I need to take care of at home," Ian said.

Harris grinned. "Yeah, I'll bet. I heard you adopted not just one but two animals from Birdie and Bunny's shelter. You do know that kids and pets don't have to come in pairs, right? You can take things one at a time."

"You know what they say." Ian shrugged. "Double the trouble…"

"Double the fun." Harris laughed. "Is that old adage really true?"

Ian answered without hesitation. "Absolutely."

As hard as the past year had been, as much as he'd felt overwhelmed by the responsibility of single parenthood to twin toddlers and despite the fact that he no longer owned a stitch of clothing that wasn't covered in dog and/or cat hair, Ian wouldn't have changed a thing. For the first time in a long, long while, he loved his life. Now what he wanted most of all was to share it with someone.

With Rachel.

He had to make things right with her. He would. No matter what it took.

"Good to hear." Harris held up a hand. "Nice running into you. Good luck with your meeting, and I hope all goes well at home."

Ian's heart lodged in his throat.

So do I.

"I don't understand." A wide-eyed Elma shook her head as Rachel opened the front door an hour later. "What's going on?"

She waved toward Rachel's modest collection of belongings, stacked neatly by the front curb. At any moment, her Uber would be pulling up in front of the house, ready to carry her to the bus station. Other than her bicycle, everything she owned fit neatly into either the blue suitcase she'd brought with her, or the second bag she'd bought to hold her books.

Rachel clutched her handbag, shut the door softly behind her and stepped out onto the porch with Elma. "I'm leaving. That's the real reason I asked you to come over. I need you to stay with the girls until Ian comes home from work."

Elma stared at her as if she'd spoken a foreign language.

"Can you do that, Elma?" Rachel prompted.

The older woman nodded, her expression a complete blank. Rachel had wondered if Elma would even be surprised by her spur-of-the-moment exit. Given how angry Ian had been when he'd come home, an anger that Elma would have seen if she'd been the one to give him the news, surely it couldn't be a surprise that Rachel wasn't staying. If she really had been lying about her credentials, Elma would likely have expected Ian to fire her. It would have been the right thing to do. She'd even wondered if Elma would look a little smug when she arrived, pleased that she'd gotten her way. After all, it had been abundantly clear that she'd wanted Rachel gone from the beginning.

But she didn't look smug. Not at all. Rachel thought she might be in shock, which she felt bad about, but she really didn't have time to stop and explain her entire decision process.

"Yes." Elma nodded. "Yes, of course. But Ian didn't tell me you were leaving. He—"

"He doesn't know, and neither do the twins," Rachel said. Her grip tightened around her handbag.

This is the hard part. Once you get through this, every member of the Parsons family will be out of your life for good.

More to the point, she'd be out of theirs—which was what mattered most of all.

"I don't understand." A deep furrow formed in Elma's forehead. "I know there were some… *inaccuracies*, shall we say…with your qualifications. But why would you leave without telling anyone but me?"

"Because saying goodbye to the girls would be

too hard. I can't do it, and I don't want to upset them. They're better off with you. I know they'll be safe, and you'll take good care of them."

"Of course I will." Elma nodded. "Why wouldn't they be...? Rachel, what is this really about? Are you sure you don't want to talk to Ian before going?"

"Ian and I did plenty of talking last night. He knows about the risk—about why I have to go. Believe me, leaving is what's best for everyone. When you tell him tonight, he'll understand. But please don't tell him until then. Promise me you won't call him." Rachel's throat closed up tight. If she didn't get out of here soon, she was going to collapse into sobs. *Just a few more minutes. You can cry all the way to Charleston once you get on that bus.*

Her bus didn't leave for several hours, but she wanted to be long gone before Ian got home. Their conversation last night had been painful enough.

"I just don't know about this," Elma said.

But then a black SUV rolled to a stop in front of the house, and the driver rolled down the window and called Rachel's name.

"That's me!" Rachel waved as the driver began piling her things into the back of the car. She turned back to Elma. "Please—I really need that promise."

"Oh my goodness." Elma pressed her hand to her chest. "This is all happening so fast. But I—I promise. I won't call Ian. I'll wait to tell him until he gets home."

"It's for the best," Rachel said. Maybe if she repeated it enough times, she might actually start to believe it.

She *did* believe, though. If she didn't truly think that moving on was the right thing to do, she never would've been able to pack her bags. But as much as she wished it was otherwise, Annie and Abby would only be safe once she was gone. Rachel's feelings didn't matter—not about this.

"Thank you, Elma." She threw her arms around Ian's mother-in-law and held on tight. "For everything."

Elma stiffened for a moment before wrapping her arms around Rachel and returning the embrace. "Please don't thank me. This is all my fault."

"No, it's not. I promise you it isn't," Rachel said, squeezing her eyes closed lest any tears should fall.

This was Frank's fault. And hers…for thinking she could involve other people—innocent people—in her messed-up life without fully considering the consequences.

Would it always be this way?

Would she never be able to grow close to someone without wondering if she was putting them in jeopardy?

Would she ever be able to fall in love again?

Rachel didn't have the answers to those questions, and wasn't sure she ever would. All she knew was that she'd already fallen in love, despite every effort not to. And now she had to do what was best for the family that had captured her heart.

It was time to find a new place to call home... until she'd eventually have to leave and start all over.

Again.

"Finally." Elma pinned Ian with a glare the second he walked through the door after work.

He froze, trying to figure out what he'd done wrong. He wasn't late. On the contrary, he'd come home a full hour and a half earlier than usual. The moment he'd finished delivering the presentation he'd been working on to his client, he'd walked straight out of his office and asked his assistant not to bother him at home. He needed to talk to Rachel as soon as possible.

Ian hadn't liked the way they'd left things. *At all.* He'd barely been able to concentrate on anything at the office—it was a miracle that he'd made it through the presentation without getting tripped up. All he could think of were the things he needed to tell Rachel. Important things. Things he should have said last night, starting with the most important of all.

I'm in love with you.

Being greeted by a livid Elma upon his arrival hadn't been part of the plan, though.

"Where's Rachel? Where are the girls?" He glanced around the kitchen and craned his neck to peer toward the front foyer. There was no sign of his nanny or his daughters anywhere. "And what do you mean by *finally*? I'm early. Did something happen? Why didn't you call?"

"Abby and Annie are fine. They're in their room with Pepper and Salty." Elma began pacing the length of the kitchen counter, wringing her hands as she moved back and forth. "I promised her I wouldn't call, but the waiting has been torture. You need to do something, Ian. You need to go after her *right now*. It's probably already too late."

Bile rose to the back of Ian's throat. He didn't know what Elma was talking about, but it sounded bad—bad enough that every muscle in his body tensed, preparing for the worst.

"Tell me Rachel didn't leave," he said, but even before the words left his mouth, he knew she was gone.

It's probably already too late.

Elma's voice rang in his head like a terrible echo. Ian didn't even need confirmation that Rachel had packed up and left. He'd *felt* her absence the minute he'd walked inside the house. The air was thick with sadness.

Too late, indeed.

"She's gone. She called me this morning and invited me to come over for a tea party with the twins, and when I got here, all of her items were stacked at the curb and she'd already called an Uber. She told me that it wasn't safe for her to stay—but she wouldn't explain what she meant. She said you would know." Elma paused her hand-wringing long enough to glare at Ian. "This is all your fault. What did you say to her?"

Ian's jaw clenched. He could have easily turned this around and blamed Rachel's sudden disappearing act on Elma. After all, she'd been the one who'd gone poking into Rachel's background. She'd been the one who, at times, had gone out of her way to make Rachel feel unwelcome. She'd also stormed into Ian's office less than twenty-four hours ago, eager to tell him that Rachel wasn't who they thought she was. Now here she stood, laying all the blame at Ian's feet.

He couldn't argue with her, though. As much as Elma had stirred the pot, Ian knew Rachel wouldn't ever let his mother-in-law drive her away. She loved Annie and Abby too much to let Elma's meddling get to her. But Ian...

His opinion mattered. As soon as they'd developed feelings for each other, Ian had the power to hurt Rachel. For a brief, shining moment, he'd held her heart in his hands, and then he'd gone and ruined everything, letting her believe that she had to face the danger in her life alone. That he wouldn't protect her *and* the twins from any threat that tried to get near them. He should have told her that they were safer and stronger together. But he hadn't. And now it was too late.

"It's complicated," Ian said quietly.

He didn't want to betray Rachel's confidence by telling Elma about her abusive ex-boyfriend. Ian had made enough mistakes lately. He didn't want to add proving himself untrustworthy to the list.

"Let's just say she had a good reason for keeping certain things about her background to herself. She didn't lie about being certified in the state of Virginia. Rachel is every bit as qualified as she made herself out to be," Ian said.

Elma crossed her arms and stared daggers at him. "I still don't understand why she would just up and leave."

Ian sighed. "Because she thought it was the only way to keep the girls safe."

"Why on earth would she think such a thing?"

Ian leveled his gaze at his mother-in-law and finally admitted the awful truth out loud. "She believes it because I told her that was the case. I was wrong, and if I could take it back, I would."

"Oh, Ian." Elma shook her head. "Then, you have

to get her back. You *have* to. Annie and Abby have been asking me every ten minutes when she's coming back. I haven't been able to bring myself to tell them that she's gone for good."

He slumped into one of the chairs at the kitchen table and dropped his head in his hands.

Think, damn it. There had to be something he could do.

"I'm sorry, son." Elma rested a hand on Ian's shoulder, and the fact that it was the first time she'd called him *son* since Serena's passing wasn't lost on him. Rachel had helped heal more than just his heart…more than his daughters'. She'd touched each and every one of them. Against all odds, she'd made them a family again. "I should've never been jealous of a woman who cared enough about your children to leave them in order to keep them safe. I promise I won't cause any more problems for the two of you."

Ian lifted his head from his hands and looked directly into Elma's eyes. "What do you mean by that, exactly?"

"Oh, Ian. It's obvious the two of you are in love. I've known for weeks."

If his heart wasn't in tatters, Ian might have laughed. "For weeks? I'm not sure I've even known that long."

"Yes, you have." Elma lifted a brow. "You just weren't ready to admit it. And if I'm being honest with us both…" She bit her lip. "I don't think I was ready, either."

He swallowed hard. "You might be right."

"Then, go get her, and *bring her home*," Elma said.

If only things were that easy.

Ian stood. He had no idea where Rachel was, but if he didn't try and find her, he'd regret it for the rest of his life. "I'll do my best. I'm such a mess right now, though, I can barely think straight."

Where should he start? He'd already tried calling her several times today and it had rolled straight to voice mail. What now? The airport? The bus station? Maybe he could call Uber and see if he could somehow find out where she'd been dropped off.

Right, because that doesn't seem stalkerish at all.

Rachel had been running for six months already. She knew how to disappear without a trace.

"If she was standing right in front of you, do you know what you'd say?" Elma asked.

So many things…

He'd tell her he was sorry. He'd tell her he'd never let anyone hurt her ever again. He'd tell her that she was safe and that she had a home in Spring Forest for as long as she wanted to stay.

But first and foremost, he'd make sure she knew exactly how he felt about her. "I'd tell her I'm in love with her."

Elma's expression went soft as her gaze drifted over his shoulder. "Well, here's your chance."

Heart pounding, Ian slowly turned his head to find Rachel standing in the open doorway with tears streaming down her beautiful face. She was clutching Annie's favorite toy to her chest like it was a lifeline.

If the little stuffed elephant had brought her back, then maybe, just maybe, it really was one.

For Rachel and Ian both.

Chapter Sixteen

Ian loves me?

Rachel held Annie's stuffed elephant against her pounding heart as her legs turned to Jell-O.

She shook her head. *No, that can't be true.*

She must have misheard or misunderstood. Ian couldn't love her. She'd just left his precious daughters without so much as a goodbye. Who did that?

Me, that's who.

The reality of what she'd done had hit her the moment her ride had pulled away from the curb. Annie and Abby had lost their mother at such a young age, and now their nanny had walked out of their lives without explaining why or making sure they knew that her departure had nothing to do with them.

Rachel knew she'd already played an important role in the twins' lives, and she knew what it was like to grow up with just one parent. She could remember feeling panicked when her father came home late from work, terrified that he might have been in an accident. She'd lost her mother. Losing her father had seemed like a very real possibility, even when she was a small child. All of her safety and security had seemed to exist on a razor-thin edge.

Ian's girls had struggled so much in the wake of their mother's death. Anything they saw as abandonment would open old wounds—Rachel knew that much, not just from her professional training, but also from experience. Leaving without telling them goodbye was the worst possible choice she could make. She'd be making things easier on herself—sparing herself the pain of the goodbyes—by making things harder on the girls instead. Ian could never love a person who'd done such a thing.

No one could.

"Sorry to interrupt," she said as shame spiraled through her all over again. "I wanted to come back and give Annie and Abby a proper farewell. Unless they don't want to see me anymore?"

"Of course they want to see you. I haven't told

them a thing yet, if it makes you feel any better," Elma said.

Relief nearly swept Rachel off her feet. She couldn't make herself meet Ian's gaze, though. If she did, she'd surely fall apart, and she still had a bus to catch once all of this was over.

"Oh, thank goodness. I couldn't decide whether I should come back, and then I reached into my handbag for my phone and found this." Rachel held up the elephant. "It seemed like a sign."

"Pepper will be delighted. She's practically adopted the toy as her own since she's been sleeping in Annie's bed." Elma held out her hand. "Why don't I go take the toy to her while you and Ian have a little chat?"

Before Rachel could protest, the older woman took the elephant and made herself scarce.

Well played, Elma, Rachel thought and then squared her shoulders to face Ian. Alone together, for the first time since their painful conversation the night before.

"You came back for the girls, then," he said. The ache in his voice nearly tore her in two. "And Pepper."

She had. But she'd also come back for Ian, above all else. She hadn't even realized it until she'd set eyes on him again.

Just one more kiss…one more touch…and then I can tell him goodbye for good.

Could she, though? She wasn't sure of anything anymore. The moment she told the truth about her past, the bottom had dropped out of her new and perfect world. Rachel didn't know how to reconcile her real self with the identity she'd created here in Spring Forest.

She wanted to—oh, how she longed to somehow stitch those two lives together. To *stay*, just as she'd intended before she'd had a chance to tell Ian she no longer wanted to move on. But she didn't see how it was possible, if staying meant hurting the people she loved.

"Ian, I…" *I'm sorry. I wish I'd trusted you enough to tell you the truth before you found out the way you did. I love you…*

He held up a hand, stopping her. Which was just as well, because everything she wanted to say, everything she felt all the way down to her marrow, seemed to be clogged in her throat.

"Before you say anything else." Ian inhaled a shaky breath. "Before you go…there's something you should know."

She shook her head as tears stung her eyes. *Don't say it again. Please don't.*

If Ian told her he loved her right to her face, she'd never be able to walk out that door again. Rachel wanted to do the right thing just as much as she wanted *him*. That's what love was all about, right? Sacrifice.

But heaven help her, her resistance was already wavering, just looking into his eyes.

"You're safe. Frank can't hurt you anymore," he said.

Rachel's head spun. What had he just said? "I don't understand."

"Come sit down." Ian pulled out a chair at the kitchen table. "Please? There's so much I need to tell you. If you still want to go after we're finished talking, I won't try and stop you. I'll take you anywhere you want to go."

Rachel hesitated. The longer she stayed in this house, the more difficult it was going to be to leave. Ian shouldn't have even been home from work already. She'd planned on returning Annie's elephant, telling the girls goodbye and getting back to the bus station before Ian knew she'd left.

But he deserved a goodbye as much as Annie and Abby did. And if there was something else he needed to tell her, the least she owed him was to hear him out. What he'd said about Frank didn't make sense at all, but it sparked a tiny flicker of hope deep in her chest all the same.

"Okay." She sat down at her regular place at the table, as if she belonged there. As if she were home.

It felt that way, no matter how much she told herself it wasn't true, that this home could never truly be hers. The table was scattered with Annie and Abby's wooden alphabet blocks, as if she'd just been stacking them into towers with the girls. A plate of the pink cupcakes they'd made sat on the kitchen counter. Pages from the coloring books she'd bought for the twins were tacked to the refrigerator door with magnets. Everywhere she looked, she was bombarded with memories, with connections.

She forced herself to look past the physical evidence of the time she'd spent in this cozy home and focus on Ian's honey-colored gaze instead. But somehow that was worse, because ultimately, this house wasn't what had brought her peace. Ian had done that. He'd been her home.

"First, I want to apologize. I should have never made you feel like you'd put the girls in danger. Your ex's behavior isn't your responsibility. It's his." Ian's eyes bored into hers with such intensity that she didn't dare look away.

Rachel wanted to believe him, but things weren't so simple. Frank and the things he'd done to her didn't exist in a vacuum. She carried the scars from their relationship everywhere she went. Some were emotional and some were physical, but each one told a story. Until she knew for certain that Frank wouldn't come looking for her, those stories remained unfinished. And as long as there was no closure, Rachel would never have a happy-ever-after like the ones in the storybooks the twins loved so much.

"Rachel, sweetheart. Please tell me you're hearing what I'm saying. None of what happened to you is your fault." Ian's voice broke, and something inside Rachel broke along with it.

She nodded, blinking back tears. "I hear you. And it's okay. I don't blame you for the things you said last night. What I told you was a shock, and of course your first concern was Annie and Abby."

"The girls are thriving, and it's all because of you. I don't know what we would've done if you hadn't come along," Ian said.

Rachel very nearly smiled. "I don't know. I think Pepper and Salty have also been a pretty good influence."

A crooked grin tugged at the corners of Ian's mouth. His lovely, lovely mouth. "And do you really think I would've dared to adopt two animals at once without your help and encouragement?"

Rachel shrugged one shoulder. She was beginning to relax, despite her every effort not to let her guard down. Hearing Ian apologize went a long way in mending her broken heart, but it didn't really change anything about her situation. She still couldn't stay—not when she'd feel the need to look over her shoulder every time she took the twins to the park or walked Pepper down Main Street.

"The next thing I need to tell you is a little more delicate." Ian blew out a breath. "I hope you don't consider this a violation of your privacy, but I did a little digging and…"

"And?" Rachel asked, throat going impossibly dry.

"And Frank James has been incarcerated for theft. He's facing felony charges." This time, when Ian smiled, it lit up his entire face. "He's got much more pressing things to deal with than trying to track you down. Sweetheart, it's over. You're safe now."

Rachel pressed her fingertips to her lips to keep herself from crying out loud.

Frank can't hurt you anymore.

When Ian had said that just moments ago, she'd been desperate to believe him—but never in a million years would she have thought it could be true. Rachel had assumed it was wishful thinking or an empty promise.

But it was real. It seemed like a dream, but Rachel's past was finally just that—her past.

She shook her head. It seemed too good to be true. "I don't… I don't know what to say."

Ian's smile softened, and the ache returned to his gaze. This time, it seemed to reach into her most hidden places—the places where her hopes and dreams once had lived, before everything turned pear-shaped and Rachel's future became something she'd always have to fear instead of celebrate. The way he looked at her was a balm, a blessing, as he slowly rose from his chair and dropped down on one knee in front of her.

"Say you'll stay," he whispered as he took hold of her hand.

Rachel couldn't utter a word. All she could do was nod.

His face lit up with a smile. "You have no idea how glad I am about that. But I want things to be different this time. I'm in love with you, Rachel. We all are—the whole family, even Elma. You're more than a nanny." Ian's grip on her hand tightened, as if he wanted to press his words into her to make sure she believed him. "You're my heart. My soul. My love."

Then his gaze flicked toward the blocks on the table and back to her. He smiled his lopsided smile she loved so much. "And if you feel the same way, then no matter what the court system decides, I don't think you'll ever need to worry about your last name being a problem again."

So much was happening so fast that Rachel could barely keep up. She shook her head and let out a tearful laugh. "I do feel the same way. I love you, Ian. And I love your girls with my whole heart. I love your dog and your cat, and Elma too. But I have no idea what you mean about my last name."

Was he saying that she should start going by Wilson again, now that she was no longer in danger? She supposed she could. She could also get her certification in North Carolina.

Rachel should have been thrilled. Getting a proper job was what she wanted most of all when she'd left Virginia. She'd worked long and hard for that state certification. Not being able to apply to have it transferred to her new home state had been a crushing blow. And now there'd be nothing holding her back. She could get a job in the Spring Forest public school system if she wanted to. Or even a hospital. Maybe she would.

None of that seemed important right now, though. What Rachel wanted most of all was to take care of Annie and Abby. She had new hopes and dreams now. A new future, and it started with the man currently kneeling at her feet.

He flashed a wink at her and then released her hand to start moving the alphabet blocks around until they were arranged into a colorful, crooked line. "I was hoping you wouldn't need to worry about your name anymore because I'd like it to be this…"

Rachel followed his gaze and took in the word he'd spelled out with the blocks.

P-A-R-S-O-N-S.

Her hand fluttered to her throat. "You don't mean...?"

"I think Rachel Parsons has a rather nice ring to it, don't you?" Ian took her hands again and pressed a tender kiss to each one. "Sweetheart, will you marry me? If you're not ready now, that's okay. We can wait if you like. We've got all the time in the world."

They did, didn't they? It seemed too good to be true. After running for her life month after month, there was no longer any rush. She could breathe again. She could live.

She could love.

Rachel shook her head. "I don't want to wait. I want our future to start right now."

Ian scooped her into his arms and stood, hugging her with such force that she could barely breathe. The room grew blurry as tears filled her eyes and the world suddenly looked like a watercolor painting, tender and luminous.

Then something prodded Rachel's leg. She looked down and found Pepper, tail swinging back and forth as she poked the elephant toy against Rachel's calf.

"It looks like I'm not the only one who's glad you're back," Ian murmured as he pressed a kiss to her hair.

Salty wasn't far behind, purring as loud as a

freight train. And where the pets went, the twins were sure to follow. Annie and Abby skipped into the kitchen next, eyes lighting up at the sight of Rachel in their father's arms.

"Miss Rachel, where have you been? You've been gone ten million hours," Abby said as she scooped Salty off the floor. The cat rested in her arms like a baby, tail swishing languidly.

"Twenty million," Annie said, her little forehead puckering.

Ian gently released Rachel so she could bend down and hug the two children. "It felt like that long, didn't it? But I'm here to stay now. I promise."

Elma scurried into the kitchen next, waving her arms and chasing after the children and animals. "Let your daddy and Miss Rachel have some private time, girls. They need to talk…"

Her voice drifted off when her gaze landed on the alphabet blocks, and then she pressed her hands to her heart. "*Parsons.* Oh my, does this mean what I think it means?"

Rachel laid a gentle hand on the older woman's arm. "Is it okay with you if it does?"

Elma cupped Rachel's face with her palms, a soft smile dancing on her lips. "Honey, it's more than okay. It's the best news I've heard in a long, long time." She winked. "Welcome to the family."

Rachel glanced up at Ian, and he wrapped his

arm around her and pulled her close while Abby and Annie scrambled into their chairs and started making a hodgepodge tower with the blocks. The *P* block skittered off the edge of the table, and Salty batted it around with his dainty paws until Pepper picked it up in her mouth and took off for the living room. The cat bounded after her, followed quickly by the twins.

Ian chuckled, and Rachel marveled at how much he'd changed in the past few weeks. He wasn't the same person who'd been on the verge of a breakdown as he'd helped her pick up the scattered blocks on the floor of the day care center. This was a new man, a healed man. And he was hers.

"Are you sure you're ready for this chaos?" he asked.

"Absolutely." She'd found her happy ending, and with it came a whole new beginning. "In joy and in sorrow, in sickness and in health. For as long as we both shall live."

* * * * *

Look for the next book in the
Furever Yours continuity,
It Started with a Puppy
by Christy Jeffries
on sale August 2022
wherever Harlequin Special Edition books are sold.

And catch up with the previous books in the
Furever Yours series:

Home is Where the Hound Is
by Melissa Senate

More Than a Temporary Family
by USA TODAY *bestselling author*
Marie Ferrarella

The Bookshop Rescue
by Rochelle Alers

and

Love Off the Leash
by USA TODAY *bestselling author Tara Taylor*
Quinn

On sale now!

#2923 THE OTHER HOLLISTER MAN
Men of the West • by Stella Bagwell

Rancher Jack Hollister travels to Arizona to discover if the family on Three Rivers Ranch might possibly be a long-lost relation. He isn't looking for love—until he sees Vanessa Richardson.

#2924 IN THE RING WITH THE MAVERICK
Montana Mavericks: Brothers & Broncos • by Kathy Douglass

Two rodeo riders—cowboy Jack Burris and rodeo queen Audrey Hawkins—compete for the same prize all the while battling their feelings for each other. Sparks fly as they discover that the best prize is the love that grows between them.

#2925 LESSONS IN FATHERHOOD
Home to Oak Hollow • by Makenna Lee

When Nicholas Weller finds a baby in his art gallery, he's shocked to find out the baby is his. Emma Blake agrees to teach this confirmed bachelor how to be a father, but after the loss of her husband and child, can she learn to love again?

#2926 IT STARTED WITH A PUPPY
Furever Yours • by Christy Jeffries

Shy and unobtrusive Elise Mackenzie is finally living life under her own control, while charming and successful Harris Vega has never met a fixer-upper house he couldn't remodel. Elise is finally coming into her own but does Harris see her as just another project—or is there something more between them?

#2927 BE CAREFUL WHAT YOU WISH FOR
Lucky Stars • by Elizabeth Bevarly

When Chance wished for a million dollars as a teenager, he never expected it to come true—especially not via his late brother's twins, who are now his responsibility. Luckily, Poppy Digby has known the twins all their lives and agrees to stay—just for a few days!—but they each find themselves longing for more time...

#2928 EXPECTING HER EX'S BABY
Sutton's Place • by Shannon Stacey

Lane Thompson and Evie Sutton were married once and that didn't work out. But resisting each other hasn't worked out very well, either, and now they're having a baby. Can they make it work this time around? Or will old wounds once again tear them apart?

SPECIAL EXCERPT FROM

HQN

Welcome to Honey, Texas, where honey is big business and a way of life. Tansy Hill is fierce when it comes to protecting her family and their bees. When her biggest rival, Dane Knudson, threatens her livelihood, Tansy is ready for battle!

Read on for a sneak preview of
The Sweetest Thing,
the first book in the Honey Hill trilogy,
by USA TODAY *bestselling author Sasha Summers.*

"He cannot be serious." Tansy stared at the front page of the local *Hill Country Gazette* in horror. At the far too flattering picture of Dane Knudson. And that smile. That smug, "That's right, I'm superhot and I know it" smile that set her teeth on edge. "What is he thinking?"

"He who?" Tansy's sister, Astrid, sat across the kitchen table with Beeswax, their massive orange cat, occupying her lap.

"Dane." Tansy wiggled the newspaper. "Who else?"

"What did he do now?" Aunt Camellia asked.

"This." Tansy shook the newspaper again. "'While continuing to produce their award-winning clover honey,'" she read, "'Viking Honey will be expanding operations and combining their Viking ancestry and Texas heritage—'"

Aunt Camellia joined them at the table. "All the Viking this and Viking that. That boy is pure Texan."

"The Viking thing is a marketing gimmick," Tansy agreed.

"A smart one." Astrid winced at the glare Tansy shot her way. "What about this has you so worked up, Tansy?"

"I hadn't gotten there, yet." Tansy held up one finger as she continued, "'Combining their Viking ancestry and Texas heritage for a one-of-a-kind event venue and riverfront cabins ready for nature-loving guests by next fall.'"

All at once, the room froze. *Finally.* She watched as, one by one, they realized why this was a bad thing.

Two years of scorching heat and drought had left Honey Hill Farms' apiaries in a precarious position. Not just the bees—the family farm itself.

"It's almost as if he doesn't understand or…or care about the bees." Astrid looked sincerely crestfallen.

"He *doesn't* care about the bees." Tansy nodded. "If he did, this wouldn't be happening." She scanned the paper again—but not the photo. His smile only added insult to injury.

To Dane, life was a game and toying with people's emotions was all part of it. Over and over again, she'd invested time and energy and hours of hard work, and he'd just sort of winged it. *Always.* As far as Tansy knew, he'd never suffered any consequences for his lackluster efforts. No, the great Dane Knudson could charm his way through pretty much any situation. But what would he know about hard work or facing consequences when his family made a good portion of their income off a stolen Hill Honey recipe?

Don't miss
The Sweetest Thing *by Sasha Summers,*
available June 2022 wherever
HQN books and ebooks are sold.

Harlequin.com

"Wait, what?" he interrupted again. "Logan worked for a
tech firm?"

Although his brother had taught himself to code when he
was still in middle school, and he'd been a good hacker of
the dirty tricks variety when they were teenagers, Chance
couldn't see him ever living the cubicle lifestyle for a steady
paycheck.

"Yes," Poppy said. "And he developed a computer program
several years ago that allowed companies to legally plunder
and sell all kinds of personal information and online habits of
anyone who used their websites. It goes without saying that it
was worth a gold mine to corporate America. And corporate
America paid your brother a gold mine for it."

Okay, that did actually sound like something Logan would
have been able to do. Chance probably shouldn't be surprised
that his brother would turn his gift for hacking into making a
pile of money.

Poppy pulled another piece of paper from the collection in front of her. "I have another statement that's been prepared for your trust, Mr. Foley."

He started to correct Poppy's "Mr. Foley" again, but the other part of her statement sank in too quickly. "What do you mean my trust?"

"I mean your brother and sister-in-law have put funds into a trust for you, as well."

He didn't know what to say. So he said nothing, only gazed back at Poppy, confused as hell.

When he said nothing, she continued. "The children's trust will begin to gradually revert to them when they reach the age of twenty-two. That's when the funds in your trust will revert entirely to you."

Out of nowhere, a thought popped up in the back of Chance's brain, and he was reminded of something he hadn't thought about for a long time—a wish he'd made to a comet when he was fifteen years old. A wish, legend said, that should be coming true about now, since Endicott had been celebrating the "Welcome Back, Bob" comet festival for a few weeks. Something cool and unpleasant wedged into his throat at the memory.

He eyed Poppy warily. "H-how much money is in that trust?"

Her serious green eyes had never looked more serious. "A million dollars, Mr. Foley. Once the children have reached the age of twenty-two, that million dollars will be yours."

HARLEQUIN

Heartfelt or thrilling, passionate or uplifting—Harlequin is more than just happily-ever-after.

With twelve different series to choose from and new books available every month, you are sure to find stories that will move you, uplift you, inspire and delight you.